MASKS
EVOLUTION

MASKS

EVOLUTION

BY HAYDEN THORNE

queerteen
QT

MASKS: EVOLUTION

Queerteen Press
an imprint of JMS Books LLC
10286 Staples Mill Rd. #221
Glen Allen, VA 23060
www.jms-books.com

Printed in the United States of America

ISBN: 9781499748703

CHAPTER 1

IT WAS TIME for Peter's "tennis lessons." I stared stupidly at the stopwatch he handed me and scratched my head. "Um—what am I supposed to do with this?"

"Time me."

"Doing what?"

Peter stepped aside and waved a hand around the room. "I'm supposed to cover every room of the house from top to bottom. You know, literally run around each room without knocking over furniture and knickknacks or breaking anything valuable. I end my run here."

I stared at him. "That's it? Seriously?" I scratched my head again when he nodded and shrugged, a sheepish grin forming. "Don't you and Trent have something like a secret underground hideout where you play with your superhero toys and dry clean your costumes and stuff?"

"Eric, my parents might be rich, but they're not billionaires. Besides, I think having a special underground lair for superhero training and stuff is cheating. We've got a lot more obstacle courses above ground. I mean, you've seen my mom's antiques. She lives for those things. I use them for agility training," Peter said with a faint blush and a devious little chuckle. "Gives her a coronary every time, but what can I do?"

I cocked an eyebrow. "Do you change your start and finish lines? After a while, I'd expect you to memorize every inch of each room. You'd be flying through your house without much of a challenge."

"The rooftops," he answered quickly and confidently. "I go way above ground and make use of the neighborhood or any given area in the city—well, outside downtown, anyway. If you happened to look up and catch sight of a weird blur flying from one rooftop to another, that'd be me. As far as maternal coronaries go, that's even worse."

I was impressed. "So—who used to time you before I found out about your powers?"

"Whoever happened to be at home. Sometimes I'd just leave the stopwatch on the mantel over there," he said, pointing at the polished mahogany mantel behind me, "and then stop it once I ended my run. The results when I did that weren't as accurate as when someone else was keeping time, but there wasn't anything I could do."

I continued to stare at him, not only feeling impressed, but moved and downright proud.

"It's really not as high-tech as you think, Eric. I'd give my soul to have all the gadgets you see in all those comic books, but life doesn't work that way." He cleared his throat. "Trent's not too happy with the lack of comic book awesomeness, actually. Even with a tricked out bike and the swanky bachelor pad he owns, he still whines about the 'lack of proper facilities.' But if it's any comfort, we do have a pretty big basement here, and that's where I mess with gadgets and stuff. Sometimes Trent joins me there since he's got his own corner of superhero stuff set up. It's just safer for him to come here and use the basement when doing undercover communications with the police department and the mayor's office. So I guess in a way we do have an underground lair—like the Bat Cave. Only not very impressive, tech-wise, and a little dustier."

"Magnifiman goes all EMO over this? Seriously?" I nearly doubled over in laughter but checked myself when I saw how serious Peter was.

"Everything about being a superhero around here—"

"Or a supervillain?"

Peter nodded. "—is purely accidental. Sucks having to grasp at straws from the get-go."

"I don't think it's accidental to those geneticists who screwed around with you guys."

He nodded again, a faint shadow of pain flittering across his features.

I gave his arm a reassuring squeeze and tried to steer the conversation away from a subject that obviously still hurt him (and maybe always would). "Okay. I get it. Why'd your mom try to make such a big deal about your hideout and training base or whatever when I had dinner with you guys? I don't see anything embarrassing in using your own house for your superhero training." I grinned. "Actually, I kind of find that cool. Everyone expects big, secret hideouts for superheroes, not run-of-the-mill houses, dusty basements, or even alleyways or whatever."

Peter shrugged again. "I don't know. I guess she wasn't sure how much you knew about me and Trent and was trying to protect us."

I'd long learned that Peter's references to going down a chute when he transformed were actually metaphorical. When he transformed, he felt like he was going down a chute—a rush of light and wind, a blink, and that was it. Calais in sexy spandex, ready to open a can of whup ass. He was totally embarrassed admitting the truth to me when I asked to see the chute. He said he wasn't sure at first what it was he was going through during the transformation process and at one point actually believed he was sliding down something. The more his powers were refined, though, the more aware he was of the process and was seriously embarrassed by his mistake.

I must admit to being at first disappointed by the reality of his transformation, but in the end, everything actually sounded pretty awesome, and I hoped to be able to watch him change someday, feeling proud all over for being chosen to be his boyfriend.

"That's cool." I picked my way through the furniture, antiques, and knickknacks, my canvas sneakers squeaking on the shiny wood floor. I stopped when I reached the mantel and turned around. "Okay, this'll be the end of the line for you. Ready?"

Peter strolled up to me, hands in pockets, eyes narrowing. "What's in it for me?" he asked, his voice dropping once he stood a few inches away.

My jeans tightened as usual. I thought I could feel my pupils dilating. Now wasn't the time to be horny, though, with the fate of Vintage City at stake. "You'll be a better superhero," I replied. I sucked as a liar, by the way.

He traced my mouth with a finger—lightly, slowly. He knew how to play dirty; he knew that I knew it; he knew that I knew that he knew it. "That's it? How boring."

"Okay, a kiss," I bleated.

He stepped back, smirking and looking a hell of a lot more wicked than I'd ever seen him. Too bad that he wasn't in superhero gear. Then again, if he were in costume, I'd have kept him from his daily agility training, and not once would I regret it, oh, no.

"I'm ready," he said, turning around to face the door.

My hand slightly shook as I raised it, stopwatch poised. "Okay. Ready—go!"

My thumb pressed the button, and Peter vanished, literally, from the room. It was a bizarre moment, and I guess I totally had to get used to it. One second his figure was there. Then there was this weird optical illusion type of thing in which his figure, or the lines of his figure, suddenly blurred, and colors mixed with each other till Peter appeared to dissolve before me. His hair, his shirt, his pants—they all seemed to drip downward, like a melting multi-colored candle, till nothing was left but empty space.

I didn't know how long I stood there, gaping at where Peter used to be, my hand raised with the stopwatch ticking away. I didn't even realize I was holding my breath till I felt my lungs hurt. I shook my head, started breathing again, and turned my attention back to the time.

"Eighteen seconds. Nineteen. Twenty. Twenty-one. Twenty-two. Twenty-three. Twenty-four. Twen—"

A flash of light, the world suddenly turning upside-down, a thump, and a stiff surface pressing against my back. I yelped, gasped, and blinked the crazy swirling room away and found myself lying on the floor in front of the mantel. Peter lay stretched out on top of me. He grinned as he took my hand and made me press the stopwatch's button.

"Twenty-five," he said. "That's a record for me. Then again, the incentive's pretty good this time."

He kissed me, and I still hadn't gotten over my shock. I felt the warmth, the softness, the moistness of his mouth and tongue, but I was still all wide-eyed the whole time, staring at the ceiling before he filled my vision with his flushed, smug leer when he raised his head to look at me.

"What the—"

"What, are you complaining?" he asked, looking almost drunk with that whole leering smugness thing. "I forgot to mention I promised my parents to do better with my time. I've cut it down by a couple of seconds, and I want to do even better. Without screwing up an antique or two."

"You broke an antique?"

He sniggered, blushing. "I did, more than once. That's why my time's much slower than what's possible for me."

"Well, at least you're working on agility and stuff, or whatever you call it when you move fast and avoid breaking things." I was growing more aware of a very happy pressure below the waist, with Peter lying on top of me like that. I contemplated raising his reward a few notches right then and there.

He stumbled to his feet, though, pulling me up with him despite my dizziness. Then he whipped out a small notebook from his shirt pocket and scribbled stuff down, no doubt the results of his run. Talk about organized. And anal retentive. Or obsessive-compulsive. Whatever. One of those, anyway, or maybe all three.

"Uh, okay," I stammered while he took his place again. "Time to beat his twenty-five seconds. Ready? Go!"

Twenty-four-and-a-half seconds went by this time, with Peter careening into the living room, snatching me off the floor and nearly slamming me against the wall when he claimed his prize.

No words could accurately capture the gratitude I felt when I realized Peter had taken care to slow down his speed by several nanoseconds (or whatever they were called in the world of hyper-speed) when he literally swept me off my feet to make sure I didn't get injured (too much, anyway) during his trophy presentation. At least my skull stayed safe because he used one of his hands to cushion it against the wall. It was the same kind of care he'd used when he'd tackled me to the floor just a few seconds earlier, come to think of it.

I must say, though, despite the shock, confusion and growing soreness all over my body, I was getting really turned on by Peter's tennis lessons. He pressed me against the wall, and I was happily giving him my own version of a Wimbledon Grand Slam Title.

We were breathing hard when we broke the kiss.

"Does this mean when we finally—you know—do it, it'll only take us half a second before it's over?" I panted.

"Ha-ha, very funny," he said. I could feel how excited he was. But I knew it was a bad idea despite the chance we had, with his family away at work and the housekeeper enjoying the afternoon off.

Sucked being me sometimes.

"So how does everyone know you actually covered all the rooms in the house? You could cheat, you know, hide in some room anywhere and wait things out for a few seconds before coming back here," I said as Peter took his place for one more lap.

My brain went into overdrive. I imagined him leaving some

kind of time warp-ish trace behind him—the same way motor-boats left a trail of bubbles or churning water in their wake—that could be detected and measured with the use of special instruments that only superheroes could invent. Maybe there was a hidden camera in each room that monitored Peter's progress with special infrared capabilities and whatever else kind of stuff those things were supposed to have.

Shifts in temperature in each room, maybe? Those could be measured as well, I thought. I was so scientific at that moment, I totally freaked myself out.

Peter glanced over his shoulder to frown at me. "I never cheat, Eric," he huffed. "Never."

"Okay, okay. Sorry. My bad." I turned my attention back to the stopwatch. "Ready! And—go!"

Poof! There went my Wonder Boyfriend. I winced and massaged my head with my free hand when a sudden stab of pain ripped through my skull. Oh, great—what a time to come down with a headache. It went away pretty quickly, though, like it never happened to begin with, and I was back to kind-of-sore-but-horny mode again.

Well, better to be prepared this time for Peter's award ceremony. I couldn't afford any more bruising, with Mom getting all suspicious about those fading marks up and down my body the day The Devil's Trill tossed me back onto my bed, passed out and screwed up. She'd forgotten to bring it up in conversation since, but I figured it was only a matter of time.

I picked a more comfortable spot in the middle of the living room, where the gorgeous Persian rug lay. I stretched myself out on it, enjoying the feel of soft, froufrou wool, hoping I looked slutty enough.

"Twenty-one," I counted, undoing the top two buttons of my shirt while I focused on the stopwatch. I went back and forth over whether or not I should undo my jeans but decided to take things slow and just wait till the next round to strip completely. That was as slow as I was willing to be with Peter.

"Twenty-two. Twenty-three. Twenty-four. You just missed your record, Peter. Twenty-six. Twenty-seven. Slacker! Twenty-eight. Twenty-nine—"

Something dark materialized above me, and it took an eternity for my eyes to adjust their focus. Little by little, details became clear. A pale, oval face, dark almond-shaped eyes, high cheekbones, dark hair pulled back in a stylish bun, designer glasses, vanilla-colored power suit. I was *so* screwed.

"Eric? Are you okay?" Mrs. Barlow asked from what looked like a massive height. Oh, shit.

"Hi, Mrs. Barlow," I said, grinning.

"I thought you fainted. What are you doing on the rug?"

"Nothing," I stammered, quickly fumbling with my shirt with one hand and pulling my collar tightly around my neck for decency's sake. I could feel the heat rising from my skin. "It's been a long day. I'm kind of tired and figured the rug would be a nice, you know, bed—sort of."

She blinked and moved away as I stumbled to my feet. Dignity? What was that?

I chuckled, raking a hand through my hair. "I didn't hear you come home."

"I just got here. I'm a quiet walker." She grinned. "Drives everyone crazy, but I can't help it. Now, are you hungry? We can have some tea in a bit. I just sent Peter out to get us something to eat. Do you like Russian tea cakes?"

"Yeah, thank you. Wait. You found Peter?"

"He found me, actually. He was about to run up the stairs when I walked in, and he stopped to greet me," she replied with a proud little smile. Waving me over, she turned around and led the way out of the living room. "He told me you're here helping him train. I really appreciate your time. Peter needs all the support he can get from everyone right now, with him coming into his powers and so on. Things have been pretty crazy with him."

"It's no problem. I'm learning a lot, too. I hope to help him and Trent and anyone else like them when the right moment comes. Well, God knows what I can offer. I mean, I'm not a superhero, and other than calling the cops and throwing a few punches when trouble comes, I don't know what else I can do. Do I sound stupid or something? I don't even know if I have good aim."

Mrs. Barlow laughed and patted my back. "No, you don't. Sometimes I wish I had the powers my sons have, so I can at least be there with them when they're being threatened. There's nothing worse to a mother than feeling helpless when her children's safety is on the line."

I nodded and thought of Mom. "Yeah. I understand."

Before long we were in the drawing room. Yep, the Barlow family actually had a drawing room, for chrissakes, and it looked just like the kind of drawing room one would find on a PBS historical drama, only modernized, even though the creepy ancestral portraits were still there. I could feel the disapproving gaze from every pair of painted eyes that watched my progress into the room. The fact I was alone in the company of my Kinda Sorta Mother-in-Law didn't help me and my growing nervousness. The fact she also walked in on me while I was making myself available to her son in the skankiest way possible nearly made me stop and puke into one of her antique vases. I hoped like hell she'd never, ever get the chance to talk to my mom.

"Mrs. Barlow, can I ask you something?"

"Of course! Have a seat, dear. Peter should be back soon." She sat on a loveseat directly across from me, leaning back and crossing her legs as she waited. With her glasses on—Peter told me she needed them for driving—she made me feel as though I were going through therapy.

"About Peter's—um—tennis lessons…"

She smiled and nodded.

"How—how do you know he actually covers every room in the house before going back to the start line? I mean, is there, like, a camera or temperature gauge or whatever hidden in the rooms that record his movements?" I scratched the back of my head while returning her smile with an embarrassed little grin.

"You silly thing," she said with a laugh. "Unfortunately, we don't live in a comic book. Life isn't that interesting in a superhero's home. When I help him in his training, he tells me which rooms he goes to. That's all I need."

"Okay."

"He sometimes goes way above ground and takes advantage of the rooftops. Did he mention that?"

I nodded.

"I guess it helps him, practicing in an environment that's basically his, um, battleground, but knowing that my boy's up there, zipping around three or four stories above the streets, gives me the hives." She shook her head. "The choices he makes sometimes…"

"And you're able to keep track of his training when he goes outside? It's a little more complicated, isn't it?"

Mrs. Barlow leveled me with an intense look. It was sudden. I wondered if I'd somehow offended her. Considering my current track record with my own parents, I wouldn't be surprised if I had. "Peter doesn't mess around, Eric. He isn't capable of being dishonest."

I nodded and dropped my gaze to my hands on my lap, wondering if Peter wasn't capable of dishonesty because he was naturally honest or if he was genetically manipulated into behaving a certain way.

"Oh, God," I whispered, mentally slapping myself and cussing like a sailor for thinking along those lines. I could be such an idiot. When I finally looked up and met Mrs. Barlow's gaze, I found her watching me with a pretty weird, unreadable expression. If I'd felt nervous walking into the room with her, I now felt downright creeped out at being examined like that. So I defaulted to my trademark dimpled smile even while I was totally shrinking, all embarrassed, in front of her.

CHAPTER 2

NO OTHER PLACE marked seasons the way Vintage City did. In short, it showed nothing other than sun and rain—more on the rain than the sun. Fog came in sometimes, too, but I think that was mostly for effect with its predictable drab grayness unless one of the factories had another accident. In that case, the fog took on a pretty interesting cast. It felt like walking through curtains of vaporized vomit, with the hospital's urgent care suddenly enjoying a boom in its walk-in patient statistics. Actually, Dad would confirm that last part because, yeah, he'd been one of those walk-in patients and almost had to set up camp there, waiting for help, because the place was packed. Too bad patients couldn't sue the weather.

Come to think of it, I wouldn't be surprised at all if my generation, having inhaled all kinds of gross chemical crap since we came into this world hairless, toothless, and broke, were doomed to give birth to three-headed babies. And then die hairless, toothless, and broke when the time came. God, what a life.

Fact was, I'd been marking the days since Magnifiman first showed up and was floored by the realization it hadn't been that long.

"No way! Jeez, it feels like forever!" I muttered, scowling at the calendar that was tacked up on the wall beside the door, one of those cheap freebies that my dad got from his job. For this year, the calendar's theme was Dogs Playing Poker, the current month being a reinterpretation using Michelangelo's style. Nice to know that Dad's hard work was appreciated.

"What was that, honey?"

"Oh, nothing." I quickly shuffled over to the dining table, where Mom had been sitting for the last half hour or so, scribbling down a list of stuff for me to buy. It was more like repeated scribbling then scratching out. "Mom, you're giving yourself a hernia writing a grocery list. What're you planning to cook tonight?"

She didn't look up. I watched the pen scratch out a couple of words, hesitate, then go back and black them out with dark, jagged lines. "Spaghetti and garlic bread," she finally said.

"I can go and get us a frozen dinner. It's no big deal. You should take it easy tonight and not even bother cooking anything from scratch."

"No, no, no, don't be silly."

"I'm serious! You look pretty stressed out and tired. Don't worry about cooking." I moved away before she could stop me. "One family-sized frozen spaghetti dinner, coming up."

Mom sighed and leaned back in her chair. "Don't get anything that's not on special this week, okay?" She pulled her wallet out of her purse, which lay in a battered lump on the table, and fished around for some bills.

"Okay."

"It's been tough lately at work, and we can't afford to be frivolous." She handed me a twenty and patted my arm, giving me a wan smile before turning away and shuffling over to the cupboards for her coffee mug. "And be careful out there."

"Okay." I smiled back at her, hoping she didn't see through me.

⚔

THE JUMPING BEAN wasn't hiring, and neither was Olivier's. It was a bit of a blow, but after further thought, I figured I didn't want to see my favorite hangouts de-glamorized from my perspective behind the counter.

My three-block walk to the nearest supermarket turned into a zigzagging six-block trek with my book bag, in which I stuffed an old folder with extra copies of generic job application forms. Where'd I get them? I kind of just snagged a handful of those things from the holder in a random store. Don't know if that counted for stealing, but I wasn't tackled by store cops at least.

It was also a zigzagging six-block trek of knocking on shop doors and looking my humblest or most confident, depending on the business. I only hoped my clothes didn't count against me as it had been a while since I'd bought new gear. Then again, I also hoped people would take one look at my second-hand fashion sense and say, "Jesus, give this kid a job!"

No one wanted me, though, and after buying frozen spaghetti and garlic bread, I was too bummed to go straight home. I wandered around for a bit, taking in the sight of Vintage City's moon face façade, which looked more like an epic case of acne cross-breeding with chicken pox. Here and there, scars from Magnifiman's battles with the Trill could be seen, despite all the money put into reconstruction and stuff. Thick steam rising through grates on the pavement barely hid the battered sections from the view of passersby.

I passed near the aerial tracks and saw that construction was close to being done. God only knew how much of the city's money went into all these repairs, but I could only imagine a near-empty treasury and our mayor still crying his eyes out over the shitty luck that kept coming his way. What the hell were those geneticists thinking, screwing around with people's babies and turning them into destructive machines? What about Vintage City, where most of them, probably all of them, still lived? We'd been lucky so far that the bystander casualties had been few, and the injuries weren't life-threatening. I sure didn't expect that good luck to last, especially once superheroes and supervillains reached the top of their game. The damage to buildings and streets was more extensive, but maybe not as extensive as it could be, when all of those genetically-manipulated kids were to come into power, for good or bad. God, I couldn't even wrap my mind around the craziness that their fights would cause.

The aerial tracks passed over the main square, and I saw that the founder's statue was still headless. Well, sort of. Someone had temporarily replaced the missing head with a pumpkin, which was well on its way to turning into organic mush, but what a gothic-looking thing it was!

I looked around, and people were too busy scurrying from one place to another to notice. Either that or they didn't care. It wouldn't surprise me if they didn't. That pumpkin up there was the fourth to be perched on the headless statue after City Hall went into one meltdown after another and had the first vegetable removed. I guess people wanted something between the shoulders of our city's founder, and a good-sized pumpkin did the job while supervisors argued over the replacement head and where to find the right source for it. I sure didn't blame the people of Vintage City. Who'd want a headless man for their founder? This time around, City Hall decided to leave the current pumpkin alone and let it rot itself into oblivion.

I made a note to swing by the square at least twice a week to check on the pumpkin's progress and see if it would be replaced by another vegetable. I hoped one of the Asian markets would donate a durian. Then we'd have a punk rocker for a founder, and that'd kick major ass. I heard that durians stank, too. That'd be way better!

"Hey! Skinny boy!"

I felt a rough tap against my shoulder and whirled around. Mrs. Zhang stared up at me from under her makeshift hat—a plastic grocery bag which she tied around her head and topped off with a garish scarf for aesthetics. Thick, colorful wool cocooned her pudgy figure against the weather, which didn't at all do her black galoshes any justice.

"Hi," I said, smiling back despite my moroseness. "Been out shopping?"

Mrs. Zhang tugged around a kid's cart—in bright yellow—stuffed with grocery bags. "Yeah," she said. "Not for restaurant, though—for home."

I suddenly felt embarrassed by the pathetic, half-filled plastic bag I carried and tried not to eye Mrs. Zhang's treasure too much. Reminders of my parents' current money issues came back, and with them were reminders of my job-hunting busts.

"Why you out late? You don't have homework to do? Or you run away from home?"

"Oh, I went to the store for my mom."

"You should go home, then. Too dangerous out here. Bad guy with kinky small assistants still loose, and two nights ago, they left sticky nose prints on my restaurant's windows. Bastards."

"Can I haul your groceries home for you, Mrs. Zhang?"

"I'm going to restaurant first. If you want, you can escort me," she said, nodding and grinning. "Though still too skinny to be any use in case of mugging. What the hell you doing? Fasting? You Catholic?"

"I started out Catholic, yeah, but I'm at a crossroads right now. I'm leaning toward Buddhism, actually."

"Huh. Trying to get on my good side. Not working. Eat more, and I won't be so grumpy with you."

I escorted Mrs. Zhang to her take-out place. We weren't mugged, and bless her, she gave me complimentary Broccoli Beef for dinner. If she kept this up, she'd be bankrupt, and I had my genetics to blame.

Mom was grateful for the freebie, but I could tell her pride was stung. "You really should turn down Mrs. Zhang whenever she does this, Eric," she said while I helped her set the table. "She's too generous, and I'd hate to eat into her profits. I know she likes you a lot and treats you like her own son, but you need to be more firm with her."

"She's only trying to be nice, Mom," I said.

She stared at me, her eyes narrowing. "I know she is. But we're not a charity case, either. Your father and I can take care of us well enough."

"Okay, okay. Sorry. I'll say no next time."

She snorted and left the kitchen. The spaghetti was in the middle of being nuked, and I carefully measured out the rice into our old rice cooker. I wish I could tell my parents about my job-hunting, but I just couldn't bring up the subject. Mom would be offended, I was sure. An occasional freebie from Mrs. Zhang's kitchen was enough to get her dander up. What more if she found out I was tiptoeing around, looking for a job because my Dad's hours had been cut back since last week, and Mom had been passed over for a promotion in favor of some brown-nosing jerk who was hired only a year ago?

I'd worked hard enough in school to raise my grades a little, but all of that time and dedication was in danger of being eaten up by a part-time, minimum-wage job that my parents hadn't approved. Of course, I'd yet to land a job, but that was neither here nor there. Better yet, I'd yet to land a job that wouldn't require parental permission because I was only sixteen, according to my state's labor laws. And that most likely meant getting something underhanded that would send me to lurking in dark alleys wearing a trench coat and a hat and selling passersby black market merchandise.

Whatever. I was determined to help out, no matter what. I'd deal with parental wrath when the moment came.

THERE'S A LINGERIE *boutique in the hoity-toity district that's looking for employees.*

"I can tell you're enjoying this," I growled at my computer screen, crossing my arms over my chest—skinny-ass chest, as Mrs. Zhang called it.

Oh, come on, Eric. Don't tell me helping women look sexy intimidates you.

"Uh, no, but I'd guess they'd freak out, seeing a boy in the middle of all that lace and silk and perfume."

But you're gay!

"Shut up, Althea."

What, aren't you?

I rolled my eyes. "It's not a good match. Is there anything else out there?"

I'll bet you you'll look good in drag. Peter agrees, but he still prefers you looking like a boy.

"What? You two have been talking about me in drag? What the heck?"

Nah. It just came up in conversation during our online game. I was trying to create a new character, and I thought of someone in drag, but somehow mutated barbarian drag queens weren't even an option when I went through my dashboard. Well, so I bitched about it, and somehow you came up in conversation, and Peter started getting a little kinky.

I could've boiled water right then and there with all the heat I must've generated, blushing. "Okay, I think we're treading Too Much Information waters here. Time to move on."

But don't you want to know what Peter said about you in makeup?

"No! Hell no! I don't do makeup!"

You used to wear eyeliner, duh.

"That's not the same."

Yeah, well, Peter loves it, in case you didn't know.

I paused. "Really?"

Really, really.

"You mean, like, full makeup?"

Eyeliner only. He said it's very 1980s. You know, I should be paid a consultation fee for gay boy beauty tips. Now, are you going to try out that lingerie boutique or not?

"Uh—no."

We're in a recession. You shouldn't be so damn picky. Okay, how about this. A little antique shop just opened up in Fourth Street. Mom and I have been there a couple of times, and I think you'll like it. It's a tiny shop, and it's crammed with all kinds of creepy old junk—just your thing, Eric. The owner's this woman who makes me think of gypsies. Like old-time gypsies that you read about in books from, like, two hundred years ago.

"She said that she's hiring?"

She complained of being the only one in the shop, so I figured she was being a little passive-aggressive on the hiring issue. Mom put a hold on a couple of chairs, you know, like a layaway thing. I can go back and put more money into it, and you can come with me to check the place out.

I mulled things over. Fourth Street wasn't too far from where I lived. It wasn't in the downtown area, which meant less traffic, but hopefully it also didn't mean less business, especially if the shop was a small one.

"Okay. Just let me know when. No one around here knows about my job-hunting, so don't say a word about it."

Wait a second! Your parents don't know? How're you going to get their permission?

"I don't intend to. If I have to, I'll forge their signatures on whatever stupid forms the school gives me," I replied with growing impatience. Damn these child labor laws! Yeah, life suckage just extended itself to the state level.

Oh, great. Your parents will have a cow, and I'll be blamed for helping you sneak behind their backs and pull something illegal.

"I promise you that won't happen."

You'll be breaking the law! You're a scummy criminal, and you're not even an adult!

"No, I'm desperate, and no one understands. My parents won't. Anyway, I gotta go. I want to turn in early tonight. It's been a long, depressing day."

You mean to say you're kicking me out because Peter's due to fly into your room and sweep you off your feet for another kinky spandex moment?

"Yeah, exactly."

Whatever. Okay, I'm going. Just don't forget the pill, all right? I'd hate to be a godmother at sixteen.

"I hope you find a boyfriend soon. Like, right now."

Don't you threaten me!

"Thanks for helping out, Althea. I really appreciate it. Now beat it."

I'm not helping you again, scumbucket! You got me this time, but no more.

"I love you, too, Honeybunch."

You suck. See you in school tomorrow.

The screen blinked and then turned black. As I tended to do after an online chat with Althea, I pushed my chair back and bent down, double-checking my computer and confirming that, ayup, the darn thing was unplugged the whole time. I shivered, all weirded out. I'd yet to get used to some aspects of Althea's powers. Communicating with her while my computer was dead was at the top of my list.

I shuffled over to my bed and plopped down, turning my attention to the antique shop. It was sure worth a try. At this point, after so many dead ends in my after-school job searches, I was willing to try anything. Well, anything but lingerie, that is.

CHAPTER 3

UNFORTUNATELY I WAS out of eyeliner—tossed the stupid thing out after I got called into the principal's office over my cosmetic preferences a long time ago. Then we had a bit of a pink eye scare in school at one point, and I refused to have anything but my glasses come anywhere near my eyeballs. Now look at me—sniffing around for something borderline carcinogenic that could cause total blindness. I'd risk shriveled eyeballs and eyelids that'd be fused shut from so many infections and for what? Yep. Funny how love worked. On my way to school the following morning, I stopped by the 24-hour supermarket for my favorite Not Even God Can Smudge This Shit Out Of Your Eyes brand, the cheap, made-for-penny-pinching-teenagers cosmetic line called Gingham Girl.

Yeah, the kind of eyeliner that needed to be semi-melted with a blowtorch before it could be used properly—not to mention, safely. The kind that was one step up from the raw stuff that could be dug up in coal mines. I bought a set of disposable lighters with the pencils and didn't really give a flying fig what the checkout girl would likely say. A boy buying eyeliner? God knew what was about to come my way.

"You know, there are better brands than this," the check-out girl—the name was Chelsea, according to her employee tag—noted, eyeing me with a tired, wan look from under scruffy blonde bangs that looked self-cut. "Softer kohl, easier on your eyes. This stuff isn't worth the savings."

All right, that one wasn't so bad. Anything would've been better than "fucking fag" hissed between clenched teeth while my change was being counted.

"Yeah, but I'm on a really tight budget right now. Maybe next time."

She shrugged and gave me the total. Two bucks. That was about one-third of the day's allowance, go me. Thank God for packed lunches. Then again, budget-y issues aside, I wasn't really too keen on downing one more plate of so-called food from the school cafeteria.

"Here's your change. Have a nice day," Chelsea mumbled, turning away even before the second word came out of her. She sniffed, yawned, and rested a hand against her lower back. I realized then she was a little bit pregnant—I meant her belly was just swelling up—in addition to looking around sixteen, seventeen tops. She abandoned her register to shuffle over to a stack of boxes, which she was apparently unpacking before I showed up. Sniffling and muttering under her breath, she picked up where she left off and pulled out all kinds of useless impulse-buy items. There were a few other employees scattered up and down the store, with no one else manning the registers or helping her out with stocking.

I glanced at my watch. It was almost seven-thirty in the morning. Jesus, what time did Chelsea start her shift? Was she even going to be in school?

LOVED MY COMPANIONS, hated my day. That was my life in Renaissance High in its abridgitated—or whatever—version, and, no, it rarely ever changed. The number two highlight of my day was my Art class. I'd long learned to gather up all my frustrations from my previous classes, and since Art was my final period, I let it rip on canvas. Or paper. Or clay. Or whatever happened to be our chosen medium for the day. Who said I needed to pay an arm and a leg for a shrink? Graphite and paint were my bestest of best friends before the final bell rang, and I always walked out of my last period feeling totally zen.

The number one highlight of my day was spending time with Peter. Naturally. That varied, of course, since he only had half an hour at most to waste before he was expected back home for his training or homework or whatnot. Some days, he'd be given the afternoon off, and we'd drive over to the Jumping Bean or the Dog-in-a-Bun or Monster Slice Pizza for a daylight date. For those days, we'd punctuate our time together with a hot, sweaty fumble till we looked like a pair of those conjoined twins in circuses back in ancient history. In our case, though, we'd be the porn version of that since we'd be so tangled up, we'd look like we were attached in the wrongest places. Imagine if God were to get totally sloshed and then went all out, building people, giggling the whole time. We'd also perform our pornographic freak show in the back seat of his car somewhere outside Vintage City, in some deserted wooded area.

"It's so thoughtful of Althea to tell you one of my kinks," he panted against my shoulder.

"What—oh, that," I gasped back, unable to move under his dead weight and the pretzel-like position I was forced into, half-lying on the back seat. My legs were tangled with Peter's, probably stuck in a square knot, or at least they felt like it. Somehow the onset of numbness from cut off blood flow did quite a number on one's perceptions. Oh, there was also the matter of our clothes being partly undone and adding to the puzzle of limb placement in such a small car. All the same, God, I felt good.

"Too bad you can't wear the stuff in school," Peter added, moving his head to brush a kiss against my temple before struggling to raise himself up a little, so he could at least look at me.

"I can on a date. A nighttime date, I mean."

He grinned and pressed down for another welcome round of kisses. Someone tried to move his legs—at this point I couldn't tell who—then Peter pulled away. "I think my legs are cramping up. Can't tell for sure. Something down there's feeling prickly."

"Yeah? I've gone past prickly down there, too. Really can't feel anything now." I started giggling insanely. "Peter, I think you'll have to make an honest man out of me."

"We haven't even gone that far!"

"We're well on our way at this rate. Better to be safe than sorry. Don't ask Father Matthew, though, or he'll give you this what-have-you-been-snorting kind of look. Hey, do Buddhists allow same-sex weddings?"

He laughed. "Jailbait. I'll have to tell your parents what—"

"Ow! Shit!"

"What's wrong?"

I pinched my eyes shut and shook my head, waiting for the pain to go away. It was a pretty sharp one, but it came and went quickly. I felt Peter shift his weight, and I opened my eyes to find him struggling to sit up, helping me move my cramped legs while I raised myself from the seat.

Silence fell for a moment as we fumbled for buttons and zippers, wiping ourselves dry first with the old towel that Peter brought with him for this purpose. It didn't take long for the pain to go away. I felt his eyes on me the whole time, and I tried to reassure him with goofy smiles as I tidied myself up.

"A headache." I sighed, slumping against the backrest once I was done.

"Do you need some aspirin or something? We can swing by a drugstore right now."

I waved a tired hand. "I'm fine, really. It's stress. Since Dad and Mom told us about their work problems, I've been worrying about them. My family." I shrugged and stared down at my hands lying on my lap. "I wish they'd let me get a job. It's not like I can't manage my time well."

"Uh, Eric, you can't."

"Okay, I can't, but I can learn. I'm not stupid." I exhaled loudly. "I don't know. Even if we weren't going through a financial crisis right now, I think I'd still fight for a job. I just—I feel so restless. All of a sudden, you know? It's been like this for a while now. Since—since the Trill got to me. I mean, I wanted to be busier before, like, get a job and stuff, but somehow it feels more urgent now."

Peter shook his head. "You've been through so many tests. Nothing's been found. I doubt if being messed around by The Trill has anything to do with your restlessness."

"I feel like I'm stuffed inside this tiny little box, and I can't move, and everything's beyond my control." I shrugged, chuckling. "Gee, paranoid much?"

"I go through that a lot," he offered. "Can't say the same about Trent and Althea, though."

"Yeah." I leaned back and stared at the car's overly clean ceiling, idly running a finger over the suede-like surface. "Maybe it's something psychological. Maybe I'm jealous that you and Althea are suddenly important heroes, while I'm just this useless average guy with nothing to offer."

He sighed and pulled me close for a tight hug. "You're in self-pity mode now. Quit that."

I smiled against his shoulder and gently rubbed his back with one hand. He was soooo warm and soooo comfy. "I guess so. I wonder if there's something I can take that'll make this urge go away. It's starting to get on my nerves."

When he drove me home, we forgot to swing by the drugstore, but that was okay. I reminded myself not to stress too much over the job thing, and my headaches should go away. I guess my physiology—or biology—couldn't really tell which was which—was being too sensitive.

⚜

SINCE ALTHEA WENT all Virtuous Good Supergirl on me, I decided to check out the antique store on my own the following day, right after school. It was hell going through the rest of my evening pretending as though I had nothing up my sleeve. Sure, I'd kept some things from my parents before, my relationship with Peter being one of them, but they were mostly small and not really important. As far as Peter went, I ended up telling them before long, anyway, and they were pretty much okay with it. They never told me not to get involved with another boy, so it wasn't as though I was going against them all the way.

I couldn't say the same thing with regard to the job thing. I was totally defying them in this case. I knew it, knew how they felt, and I still kept at it. I hated lying to them. Father Matthew might say it was a sign of a healthy Catholic conscience, but it sucked all the same. I figured I was in for some pretty nasty karma in my next life.

I must've sat on my hands and stared blankly at my plate throughout dinner. Talk around the table centered on the Bad Guy du Jour, with The Trill momentarily out of the way. Dad had the afternoon paper with him this time.

"Do you really need to read that now? It's dinner time," Mom said, scowling as she set the pitcher of water down before taking her place.

"I know, Maggie, I'm sorry," Dad replied from somewhere behind the crumpled pages he held up like a shield against the rest of us. "It's just...I saw the headlines when I passed by Sam's newsstand, and I couldn't help it."

"Well, can't you try to help it till after we eat?"

"Wait, wait—listen to this. The new supervillain's starting to leave little calling cards now, and I'm not talking noseprints from his bizarre little sidekicks."

Liz and I exchanged surprised looks. "You mean he's started his own crime spree?" she asked.

"It's about time," I piped up.

"It's a pretty freaky thought, but I have to agree with goofy goth kid here," my sister continued, jerking her head in my direction. "I hate it when they wait and make us sweat, not knowing what they're up to. Better to get all the poisons out now and be over with it."

"Which is way more than what we can say when you're PMS-ing. And for the billionth time, I'm not goth."

Liz stared daggers at me. "Mom, is it too late to put Eric up for adoption? I'm sure the SPCA's got plenty of room."

"Eric, don't bully your sister," Dad cut in, turning a page while keeping the paper held up high. "Here's more. He's identified himself as the Shadow Puppet, and—"

"See, why can't supervillains wait till Bambi Bailey christens them with something pretty horrible?" I asked.

"They're smarter than the good guys, I guess." Liz chuckled then took a few sips of water. "They'd rather not get cornered by some local reporter with bad naming habits. I'll bet you that means something."

"Oh, give me a break. They name themselves right off the bat because that's how criminal psychos are—narcissistic in epic proportions. They can't get over themselves," I retorted.

Mom sighed, looking resigned to a somewhat disrupted meal. "Eric, for heaven's sake, eat something with substance. Here, have a baked potato."

"Aww, Mom…"

"Don't you argue with me, mister."

In addition to the butter-drenched baked potato—I could've sworn Mom spread half a stick of butter on that thing—a couple of thick slices of meat loaf mysteriously appeared on my plate. I hated meat loaf with a searing, all-consuming passion, but couldn't come up with a good enough excuse for skipping it, especially now everyone knew my non-Catholic leanings. Didn't know why the Catholicism thing would matter, anyway, seeing as how everyone in this household was non-religious and bound for Hell, according to the Vatican. But apparently I was a special case, and the shadow of religion would loom over me like a stinky, black cloud. Because guilt porn.

"I'm not done here," Dad snapped. Everyone fell quiet and stared at him, or, rather, his hands gripping the afternoon paper. In fact, I think no one saw any other body part of my dad during the meal. "As I was saying, Shadow Puppet and his, uh, puppets have begun their crime spree. They've cleaned out jewelry stores and left calling cards at the crime scenes."

"Calling cards?" Mom echoed. Without skipping a beat, she buttered another steaming potato and dumped it on my plate. She ignored my high-pitched whine. I swear I sounded like a pig getting slaughtered, but did she care about my pain? Nope. "Literally?"

"He's a little more high maintenance. He leaves small dolls—six-inch wooden puppets—with messages written on their bellies."

Liz made a face. "That's creepy."

"They actually don't vary much," Dad continued. "The messages are mostly 'Gotcha! XOXO, the Shadow Puppet' or 'Bunch of losers! XOXO, the Shadow Puppet' or 'You're not much of a challenge, are you? XOXO, the Shadow Puppet.'"

"And where's Magnifiman or Calais or Spirit Wire the whole time?" Liz demanded. "Looks like they're losing their touch."

"Uh, maybe they've got their own ways of nabbing the Puppet? Duh?" I retorted.

"Like how? Let him get away with hundreds and thousands worth of jewelry and cash? Yeah, great crime-fighting method there."

I hated it when Liz, or anyone, for that matter, got all smartass-y about superheroes. How about injecting them with all kinds of radioactive or genetically-manipulated crap and then dumping them out into the streets? Let's see them cope with their mutated biological makeup and then figure out the best way of handling scum. Let's see them get all smartass-y then. People always thought it was so easy being a superhero. Armchair critics are so lame.

I came this close to shooting my mouth off and blowing Peter, Althea, and Trent's cover.

Instead I stuffed my mouth with an unhealthy chunk of Cardiac Arrest Potato and gnawed on it to bring my anger down. And my life expectancy, for that matter.

"You know," I said after swallowing the vile stuff, "pride comes before a fall. I'll bet you The Shadow Puppet and his little army of kinky dolls are bound to slip big time, with all this chest-thumping and stuff. I'll bet you."

"Actually, here's the most recent message the Puppet left: 'Don't bet on anything. I'm not that easy to figure out. XOXO, the Shadow Puppet,'" Dad said.

Forget it. "Mom, I'm full. Can I be excused?"

"Well, you didn't finish your dinner, Eric. Are you okay?"

"Yeah, of course! Why shouldn't I be?" Other than how I'd be lying to her and Dad about my extra-curricular activities starting—well—whenever I got hired? "I've got homework. Lots of it."

"All right, honey, go ahead. It's Liz's turn to wash the dishes, anyway."

I turned to Liz with a triumphant grin. "Thanks, Mom. I'll dump the trash tomorrow morning on my way out."

PETER STOPPED BY that evening. That would make it our second date for the day, and I totally reveled—hell, I swam: backstroke, breaststroke, butterfly, etc.—in my good fortune.

"Ten minute break from crime fighting," he said as he swung himself through my bedroom window, landing softly on the floor. "And I can't cheat, either. Trent's got himself a new watch, and he's using it on me. Did I mention that it's tricked out?" He shook his head, clucking. "My brother's got this love affair with gadgets. It's crazy."

"Tell him to chill out." I laughed as I embraced him. "He's

had girlfriends before, hasn't he?"

"Yeah, but they never lasted. Trent's too Type A for them, apparently."

We used to perch ourselves on the window ledge, facing out, our legs dangling. Unfortunately, we'd also be sitting ducks for target practice from some good-for-nothing, genetically-manipulated thug, and we learned our lesson from The Trill. No, it didn't stop Peter from taking a few minutes off his street-cleaning to spend time with me, but at least we took to sitting on the floor and out of view, our backs resting against furniture while we talked. If I had a camera, I'd have a dozen or so pictures taken of this superhero in full gear sitting on my bedroom floor, legs stretched out or crossed, hands cradling the back of his head as he joked and listened. Sometimes we'd be sharing an illicit soda and challenging each other in a burping contest. Half the time we'd simply be making out, with me fighting a hopeless battle against temptation as I forced my hands from pawing away at Peter's uniform.

We stayed chaste that evening, largely because Peter seemed a bit put out. Office-related stress, I'd say.

"It would be nice to meet him and your dad sometime," I said.

"They've been busy," Peter replied, glancing at me. "The Puppet's been driving Trent insane, even more so than the Trill."

I watched him. "Uh-oh. Bad night at the urban office again?"

Peter sighed heavily and shrugged, dropping his gaze to his hands as they busied themselves with brushing dirt off his spandex-covered legs. "You know what they say about shit traveling downhill. When Trent gets pissed off, it affects me, and I find it a little hard to keep my mind on my work. We've been arguing since we went out to look for the Puppet."

"I understand. Sorry if I sound whiny. I guess I get a little nervous about this sort of thing."

"Like what?"

"Like, I wonder why they haven't made arrangements to meet me, you know?" I rubbed the back of my neck. Boy, this was embarrassing to admit. "I mean, I can't help but wonder if I did something wrong to turn them off the idea or make them—you know—drag their feet and so on."

Peter sighed again as I slid closer to him. "Eric, you didn't do anything wrong. Quit that. It isn't you that's holding them up. It's their work that's getting in the way. Okay?"

"Okay, okay. I'm sorry. I just needed to get it off my chest somehow. I know it sounds stupid and all, but better to make an ass of myself to you than hold everything in, right?" I listened to myself talk the whole time and was even more horrified at the way my voice sounded so thin and weak.

"Listen to me. You're fine. There's nothing to worry about. When Dad and Trent say they're ready to meet you, I'll let you know as soon as I can. I promise."

I nodded, all deflated. Embarrassment and shame with a dash of self-loathing; I wasn't in a very good frame of mind. Noting an edge of impatience in Peter's voice didn't help me at all.

We ended our date in mildly uncomfortable and distracted silence, and when Peter moved to say goodbye, I felt relief in the air.

"Are you coming by tomorrow?" I asked as I followed him to the window.

He clambered up and glanced over his shoulder to look at me as he crouched on the window ledge. "I don't know. Just leave your window open unless it's cold."

"You'll knock if you see it's closed, right?"

"Yeah, yeah, sure."

Peter sounded pretty dismissive and curt, and I hesitated for a second. "Hey, Peter?"

"What?" he barked, looking back at me again while exhaling through clenched teeth.

"Nothing," I stammered. "Sorry. Go on. I don't want to keep you."

He gave me one last look of exasperation before leaping away into the night. I watched him go and stood at the window for several moments after he vanished.

"Sorry."

PETER WAS STILL distracted the next day, and I assumed superhero work was beginning to get under his skin, at least more deeply than it had before. I tried to cheer him up with stupid jokes and quiet lovebird conversation, but he didn't have patience for any of it.

"Look, just give me some space," he said at lunch time. "I need a little bit of that sometimes, you know. I'm sure you do, too."

I looked at Althea in some confusion, and she shrugged while stuffing her mouth with soggy French fries.

"Okay," I said and kept quiet for the rest of the day, keeping a wary eye on Peter as he brooded his way through class after class. His mood didn't change, so we ended the day with our personal space more forcefully defined. I kissed him after Art class, but it was nothing more than a fleeting peck on the cheek as he hurried to get the heck out of there.

"I guess superhero work's getting a little too hardcore lately," I noted glumly, toeing the ground as I waited for Althea to gather her stuff from her locker.

"I wouldn't be surprised," she replied. "Peter can be too intense for his own good sometimes. Hey, let's have coffee this week. Forget Barlow."

That sure perked me up. I met Althea's gaze, warming up when she grinned at me. "Sure thing. Just let me know when you're not busy getting literally wired up."

"Hell, yeah! Just because I'm leveling up in my powers, it doesn't mean I don't have time for you." She gave me a painful punch in the arm, making me yelp. It was just like old times, and I loved it.

I must've been a hell of a lot more stressed out than I first thought. I made a beeline for home because my headache returned, and I nearly emptied out the aspirin bottle. My job-hunting would have to wait one more day—an annoying thought, but what could I do?

I went to bed but couldn't sleep right away. I tossed around under my blankets, a weirdly sluggish but restless feeling coming over me, and it wasn't food-related. I even went to the bathroom a couple of times in case dinner was doing a number on my system, which it sometimes did, especially when Mom force-fed me all kinds of gross stuff. I eventually fell asleep, but I dreamed a lot—mostly strange, random images of me walking through this weird, endless maze of corridors lit by candles, following a voice I didn't hear but rather felt. Eventually I ended up in a large ballroom of some kind, packed with people dancing and drinking. All of them were dressed in elaborate costumes, sort of like in those pictures I'd seen about the Venetian Carnival.

Then the dream ended, and I woke sometime in the middle of the night, feeling more tired than ever. Not only that, I also woke to find myself downstairs, curled up on the couch. With only a T-shirt and boxers on, I was shivering, but I was much more freaked by the idea that stress had now caused me to sleepwalk.

I fumbled my way through the dark and back up to my room, wondering what had just happened, and thanking the stars that I didn't fall down the stairs while walking in my sleep.

"Damn," I muttered as I pulled the blankets over my head. "I swear to God, if it's not one thing, it's another."

CHAPTER 4

IT WAS JUST my luck, yep, that a craptastic night had to come before the day of my super-secret job application. Which was already delayed to begin with, naturally. I could barely keep my eyes open, let alone get my brain working.

What an awesome first impression I'd make.

"God, Eric," Althea said, her brows knitting, when I half-dragged myself to my locker a few minutes before the first bell rang. "What the hell happened to you?"

"Didn't sleep too well last night." I pressed my forehead against my locker and stared at it for several moments. "What's my combination again?"

"I don't know. Am I supposed to?"

"Can you do your superpower thing on it, so I can get my books?"

"Dude, I don't do primitive mechanical stuff, only computers."

I sighed, sagging against my locker and shutting my eyes. "I want to sleep right here. Maybe I should just skip the whole day and do that since I can't get to my damn books."

"Here, let me," a quiet voice said from behind.

Before I knew it, I felt myself being pulled away from my locker, held steadily though I wobbled on my feet, while a hand appeared, gave my locker handle a tug and a sharp yank, and tore the thing open.

"Oh. Shit. Sorry. I don't know my own strength."

"That's...nice," Althea stammered, pursing her lips. "Look, Eric, you can get to your books now."

I could only stare at the locker door that now hung on one hinge, slightly bent in a couple of places, the lock itself completely mangled and torn up. From within, my books and spare sweater snuggled against each other in a timid little cluster.

"Peter..."

"I'll go to Mr. Dancy's office and tell him that I screwed up your locker," Peter offered before I could go on a cosmic-sized freak out. His other hand, which held my left shoulder, gave me a gentle squeeze.

"What's wrong, Eric? You don't look too well."

"I feel like crap. I'm tired, and I'm cranky. And my stupid locker's a mess." I brushed off his hand and yanked my books out, cursing under my breath. *And I have to apply for a damn job this afternoon, while my parents think I'm at a meeting with the Quill Club,* I added silently.

"Peter's going to have it replaced," Althea said, her brows rising. "Just chill, Eric."

"Oh, for chrissakes..." I'd slammed my locker shut, only to have the battered door tear off its second hinge and fall to the floor with an obnoxious clatter. "Hell! Peter, I can't believe you did this!"

Peter abandoned his spot behind me and bent down to retrieve the door. He looked at me with an irritated little frown. "I'm going to get this fixed now. Not later. Now. Okay? Calm down."

"You'd better. Thanks to you, I've got to take all of my books out and drag them all over the place, just to make sure no one steals them out of my locker. Why can't you just leave things alone? I would've remembered my combination eventually, and I don't need this added stress."

Peter's frown shifted to amazement and then that familiar look of hurt, which passed quickly enough into cold calm. It was sure a good reflection of how I felt when he snapped at me the previous day—and the night before that. "Fine. I'll see you whenever I'm done getting this looked at."

"Yeah, fine." I didn't spare him a glance while I pulled book after book out of my locker, stuffing my already stuffed bag with more weight. I heard Peter turn around and walk away, and for a second or two, I actually felt bad for snapping at him, but whose fault was it, anyway? I sure didn't ask him to help me out, let alone rip the door off its hinges.

"You know, he was only trying to help," Althea said.

"I don't care. I never asked him. And he really should know better than to use his superpowers for ordinary stuff like this. It's stupid and pointless, and it'll only get him into trouble with his identity." I gritted my teeth as I hoisted my bag up, cursing all the more at the crazy-ass weight I was now forced to carry around with me.

"I don't know if it's even crossed your mind that maybe he can't help it. He hasn't gotten that far with his powers, you know."

I rolled my eyes. "Oh, and I suppose he's told you that, too, when you guys get together and gossip about me and bond over CG barbarians."

"Man, I hope you're not going to cop an attitude all day because I'm this close to kicking your ass."

"Althea, as long as people leave me the hell alone, I won't be copping anything. Okay?" I shot back, wincing under the weight of my bag as I moved off toward the stairs. "And why is it that, all of a sudden, I'm not allowed to get pissed off, while he can tell me to back off without anyone reminding him of how I feel? Huh? Why is that?"

Althea didn't say a word in return. In fact, she didn't care to talk to me for much of the day and instead hung out with Peter, who kept a safe distance from me even if we were standing or sitting, like, about two feet apart.

He was cold and aloof though we did exchange a few words here and there, whenever necessary. Whatever. Whatever, whatever, what-the-fucking-hell-ever.

I didn't know what he said to the custodian and the principal's office about the broken locker door, but he told me to see Mr. Dancy before going off with Althea after school, so I could be assigned a new locker.

"Okay, thanks." I watched Peter as he gathered his things when the final bell rang, neatly replacing books in his locker. I didn't know how I managed to get through the day with only half a brain working and less than zero sense of humor at all, but I somehow did, and by the time I caught up with Peter at his locker at the end of the day, my anger had already gone away. I suppose Art class helped, too. My sketch pad was completely obliterated by the time I was done with it.

"By the way, what did you tell him?"

"What, does it matter? I got you a new locker. That should be enough."

I winced. He didn't look at me the whole time, but I guess I asked for it. The way he bit off his words, one would think he hated talking. Exhaustion was easily giving way to some serious guilt despite that little voice in the back of my head insisting that he'd hurt me, too, and he never apologized for it. I spotted his denim jacket, which he'd crammed inside his locker.

"Did you want me to take your jacket home?"

"What the hell for?" He still avoided looking at me.

"Well, maybe it needs a wash or something."

"It doesn't."

I rubbed the back of my neck and looked down at my faded sneakers. "Hey, listen. I'm sorry I was such a dick to you this morning. I really wasn't feeling good, and…"

Peter slammed his locker shut and turned to face me, finally. "Eric, go to Mr. Dancy and then take care of the locker thing. Quit wasting your time with apologies."

I watched him hoist his backpack over his shoulder and take a step away. "Okay," I said, withering. He nodded and turned around. "Thanks." I was sure he heard me, with his acute hearing powers and so on, but he gave no sign that he did. All the same, I took advantage of it as he continued to walk away and hissed, "I wish you'd quit being so sensitive. You make me feel like I'm not allowed to be anything but upbeat and snuggly, twenty-four hours a day, and that's really unfair. Then again, I guess I shouldn't bitch about it. I'm not a super-hero, after all. I've got no right to complain about anything."

He continued to ignore me, and I walked off to find the school custodian. Before long, I'd lightened my load into my new locker and was soon sitting in Althea's car, nervously chewing on a nail while we inched our way through sluggish traffic toward Olivier's, which was a couple of blocks from Fourth Street. I'd told her to drop me off there, adding falsehood to my friend to my growing list of sins. Once she left, I was going to walk on down to the antique store and take care of the job thing. I was sure I looked like crap. I seriously felt like it, with depression and fatigue taking complete control of my reality.

Althea said nothing the whole time. She wasn't as cold as Peter was, but she still held back, and I suppose I couldn't blame her. I tried to draw her into some kind of conversation— at least to show I didn't mean to be a jerk and to let her know that I wasn't pissed at her or Peter. Okay, I wasn't pissed at her.

"You know what? I was just thinking. Wouldn't it be crazy if any of our teachers turned out to be another supervillain or even a superhero?" That was lame, but it was worth the effort, and it worked.

"Can't be," Althea said, her eyes glued to the road. "All the genetically-manipulated babies fall within a certain generation. Remember? The labs weren't around long enough to screw around with people from a bigger age range."

"I forgot about that. So I guess it would be people from our age group all the way to Trent's, right?"

She nodded. "Yup. Which can only mean it's going to be a long, long battle we'll have ahead of us. If you consider everyone's ages and life expectancy and all that. Then again, I'm still not sure if anyone's vulnerable to serious injuries and death."

"I guess, in a way, I'm hoping the good guys are invincible and the bad guys aren't," I said.

"I know. All things being equal, though, that's not going to be possible. I've got a feeling that both sides are invincible..."

"God. I don't think Vintage City can survive that."

Althea shot me a worried look. "I was thinking that, too. If anything, it's just as bad as the thought that people with superpowers can be hurt and killed."

My blood froze, and it took some doing for me to brush the possibility off my mind. I continued to chew on a nail while mentally measuring the shortening distance between us and the antique store. We turned a few more blocks, forced into a couple of detours that got Althea snarling and blaring her horn till I wondered if I should simply get out of her car and walk the rest of the way.

"Is there anything you can hack into that'll get everyone out of our way? You can force everyone into a detour and free up a few side streets for us," I suggested, my head throbbing now from a different kind of pain. I expected my brains to ooze out of my ears at any time, taking bits of skull bone with them.

"You really think like a criminal. Stop that. Anyway, we're almost there."

"Well, that blows. You mean to say I can't convince you to hack into the school computer and change my Geometry grades?"

"Eric, shut up."

I sighed as we turned the final corner into a quiet, nearly deserted side street that would lead us to Olivier's.

"Hey, listen, do you think—"

There was a sudden flash, and the street ahead appeared to be sliced in half by a thick, bright red, fiery streak. It came from above us, from the direction of the tops of the buildings to our right, and tore through the air in a diagonal line that ended its descent on the grimy asphalt with a loud *choom!* Debris flew from the impact, much of it raining onto the car.

"Shit!" Althea cried, turning the wheel so sharply that we almost spun out of control.

"Oh, crap!" I pinched my eyes shut and clung to the dashboard, bracing myself against my seat and hoping the seatbelts were enough to protect us. I felt the world spin, and my stomach lurched.

"Hold on, Eric!"

The tires continued to screech, and I banged my head against the window pretty hard. In the blackness behind my closed eyelids, the crazy feeling of a swirling world eventually stopped, and then everything went still. I slumped against the dashboard. My seatbelt dug into my lap but had slipped off my shoulder.

I raised my head and blinked away the dizziness and mild nausea and turned to look at Althea. She sat with her hands still gripping the wheel in a white-knuckled hold. She looked frozen in terror or shock, her eyes wide, her glasses hanging crooked on her face, her mouth gaping. The car was facing the wrong way, too, with its rear end resting on the sidewalk. Good thing there were no pedestrians around when the car spun out of control, but people were now appearing here and there, creeping out of alleys and dingy little shops or peeking out of rundown windows from the upper-floors of apartments.

"You okay?" I stammered, slumping against the back rest. My head felt like it had just been run over by a stampede of hippos. I gingerly felt around my right side and felt a small lump. "Oh, great."

Althea swallowed loudly and removed her hands from the wheel. "Damn it," she hissed. She fumbled for her seatbelt and unlocked it, nearly kicking the door open as she fought to get out of the car.

I did the same and stumbled around the car to stand beside her.

"Holy cow," we both breathed.

A burnt hole in the road met our gaze. It wasn't a big hole—about the size of a manhole—but it looked pretty scary all the same. The ragged edges of the crater were blackened, the depression itself oozing dirty, gray smoke. Small tongues of flame flickered in spots, with some of the asphalt debris on the road also on fire.

"Where did that come from?" Althea said, and we both looked up.

On the rooftop of the nearest dingy tenement, a figure watched the street. More specifically, a figure leaned over the edge, both hands raised and pressed against each side of the head in a gesture of shock.

"Althea," I began, giving her a nudge. "Look…"

"Hey! You! Up there!"

The figure above us snapped out its shocked trance. Its hands came down and rested on the ledge. A voice—light, nervous, and female—broke through the hollow silence.

"Ohmigawd!" she cried. "I'm so sorry! I didn't mean to hit your car! I'm sorry! I haven't gotten a hang of my fireballs yet…I lost control!"

"Fireballs?" I echoed, blinking. "You mean—"

"You guys okay? Oh, shit. I should've practiced outside the city! You two okay? I'm really sorry!" she whined. She actually wrung her hands while she apologized.

Althea and I exchanged confused glances before looking up again, but the figure had vanished.

"Damn it!" I grabbed Althea's hand and gave it a tug. "Come on! She's probably running toward the back alleys!"

We both broke into a run, with me wincing and biting back little grunts of pain with every step. "What the hell do you think we can do?" Althea demanded in breathless pants. "She's either another superhero or another supervillain, and neither of us is equipped for a standoff!"

"I'm not looking for a standoff, dummy!" I snapped back as I led her through an alley. The nauseating smell of gross, stagnant water, neglected garbage, and rotting brick bore down on us as we plunged into the shadowy area. "I don't think she's a villain. I didn't sense that from her."

Alternately running and slipping over slimy ground, we eventually reached a dead end, with no sign of the girl anywhere. I felt sick from the strain and the godawful smells that seemed to thicken around us.

"I figured as much," Althea said as she paced back and forth, scanning nearby windows and rooftops for signs of the girl. Then she finally stopped, shaking her head. "Damn! If she's another superhero, there's no way we can catch her."

I couldn't say anything. I was too busy bending forward and resting my hands on my knees as I let my stomach settle. I breathed raggedly through my mouth, my body heaving. Something felt wrong. The nausea itself didn't seem, well, normal. I straightened up, my mouth clamping shut when another sickening wave swept over me.

"Come on, Eric, let's get out of here. We'll have to meet with Peter later and tell him about this. Right now, I guess we'd better call the cops."

I nodded and tried to say something, but instead, I doubled over and violently threw up.

CHAPTER 5

WAS IT MY imagination, or was Bambi Bailey looking just a wee bit heartbroken when she appeared on camera that evening? Her hair had been freshly roasted at an expensive salon. Check. Her eye makeup looked to be about seven layers of color thick, with about five barrels of mascara adding impossible length to her lashes, so much so that one could feel the air currents from her blinking at twenty paces. Check. Her mouth appeared to be in danger of being glued shut by her lipstick, which was probably worn down to an atom-sized nub in one use. Check. Her dress gave us a pretty obvious look that included a mix of glamour, professionalism, and female vulnerableness. Vulnerablitis. Vulnerabilism. Fuck, whatever. Check.

For all those extra touches, though, she looked a little too glum as she reported on the day's news. She was like a totally painted up sadface emoticon.

"Even as Vintage City scrambles to make heads or tails of the elusive Shadow Puppet, another mysterious figure chooses to make itself known—this time through fire power. Literally."

The scene switched to earlier interviews she'd made with

witnesses. One after another, freaked out, confused, or seriously stoned folks who lived up and down that side street spoke to the camera.

"I don't know what it was, but it looked like lightning, all lit up with fire," a small, thin woman stammered. I could barely hear her with all the noise her sickly-looking baby made as she tried to calm it against her shoulder.

"It was a UFO. Or some kind of debris from a satellite," a wrinkled and grizzled man barked, spittle flying all over. Ew. "Those goddamn government experiments again."

"It wasn't a comet, was it? No? Too small?" a tall, freckled kid with bad teeth and a missing chin asked.

"Who the hell cares? It was like the Fourth of July around this dump!" a glassy-eyed girl hummed happily, her clumpy, dirty hair barely covering bruises on her face.

The camera shifted back to Miss Bailey. "No consensus among the residents of Mina Lane, though all have agreed it was a girl—quite young—who might have caused the damage. Sgt. Bone of the Vintage City Police Department has yet to make a comment about this new development." She paused and glanced up at the sky, sighing and sulking all the more when her hopes were again disappointed. She looked back at the camera. "No word yet from Magnifiman regarding the incident. In fact, we've had no word from Magnifiman in a while." She sighed again. It was painful to watch journalism going through a romantic crisis. "Is this new figure a hero or a villain? Only time will tell. For Channel 3 News, this is Bambi Bailey reporting."

"Someone should send her flowers or chocolate or something," I piped up when a commercial came on. "Or maybe romance books with those cheesy-ass, totally unrealistic covers that should be used to line litter boxes with." I'd always thought those horrible romance novel covers, when used that way, could induce cats to pee and poop and solve all kinds of health problems related to digestion and all that.

"Ssshh." A hand suddenly pressed against my forehead.

Then it moved to the side of my face and then my neck. "You feel a little warm, Eric."

"That's because I'm being roasted alive," I whined, squirming under the two layers of fleece blankets that Mom thought to giftwrap me in since the moment I returned home from my messed up job application adventure, pale and dizzy, my stomach completely gutted of its contents. Two job-hunting delays in a row over bad health—not exactly a good sign, was it? Was that some great cosmic hint that I was doomed to be on welfare when I reached eighteen?

"I know what a fever feels like. Don't be sassy with me."

"Mom, I feel like a mutant burrito."

Liz snickered from where she sat on the floor, leaning against the couch and stuffing her face with popcorn. "I'd hate to think what kind of sauce would bring out your flavor."

"Puke, most likely."

"Eric, don't be disgusting," Mom said. She shifted and stood up. "Have you finished your homework?"

"No. I was too busy imploding all afternoon."

"You mean, exploding."

"Yeah, that, too."

She sighed and gestured for me to stand up and follow her. "Come on. Let me give you something for your fever. If you still have a temperature in the morning, I'm calling your school."

I was about to argue against the whole fever issue but decided to keep myself in check. After further thought, I suppose it would be a good idea for me to stay home, away from as many people as I possibly could, even Peter. He was probably still sore at me, seeing as how he'd yet to return my calls—all four of them, and all done within ten minutes of each other the very moment Althea dumped me on our doorstep, weak, heaving, and miserable. I gave up after the fourth message. The ball was in his court now, and if he refused to acknowledge my existence with one measly phone call, I guess that would be that.

Seriously, I thought people broke up over worse things than

a battered locker. All the same, I did feel hurt. I'd tried to apologize and make amends earlier, but he kept brushing me off.

So what if we were in the other's shoes? Would he expect me to accept his apology? Hell, yeah! Would I? Of course! Unfortunately, we weren't in each other's shoes, and I was the one who kept getting short-changed. Love sucked. If I wallowed too much in self-pity, I felt I earned the right.

I shuffled after Mom and plopped myself down on a chair once we were in the dining room, the only part of my body enjoying some ventilation being the top of my head. My stomach still felt gutted and raw, and I couldn't stand the sight of food or drink despite Mom's attempts at getting me to take something. I was in for some pretty nasty medication, I was sure, but I suppose it wouldn't hurt me to swallow a pill or two.

"So, what do you think you ate today that made you sick like this?" she asked as she bustled around, moving from cupboard to cupboard and then the sink. I tried not to follow her movements for fear of more dizziness.

"I don't know," I said. My words came out muffled against the blankets. "I ate what you gave me."

She glanced over her shoulder to glare at me. "Are you criticizing my cooking again?"

"No, just telling you the truth."

You don't need anything—just rest. Yes, rest.

"Mom, I don't need anything. I just want to lie down. Can I go now?"

"Wait. Just take this. It's a fever reducer." She walked over to the table and set down a glass of water and a green gel cap the size of a minivan on steroids.

I stared at it. "Am I supposed to swallow that thing?"

"Eric..."

Now, now. Don't argue. The poor woman's only doing her best by you.

I sighed and forced the pill down my throat, emptying the glass in a few large gulps. I grimaced at the feel of so much water chasing after a gigantic capsule. "Can I go now?"

"Okay, go ahead. I'll check up on you in a bit."

"Thanks, Mom." I stood up and shuffled away. The suffocating heat that wrapped around me made my discomfort even worse. It even seemed to make my broiled brain hear voices, or make me hear voices from my broiled brain. Whichever way I looked at it, it was me and my brain—which was broiled—and we were having a really fascinating conversation.

"Oh, look," I muttered dejectedly as I checked my answering machine. "Still no call."

He might be busy, running around the city and looking for Miss Firestarter. Or even the Shadow Puppet.

"Yeah? Well, I guess that's okay. As long as he's not too pissed at me."

He might very well be, but he'll get over it. Forget him for now. Just rest. You need it.

I climbed onto the bed, dragging the blankets with me. I burrowed under the bedcovers till I was literally buried under four layers and flailing weakly as I struggled for breath.

You don't really need the extra blankets.

I gasped when I managed to surface, my breathing ragged. "Okay, if you want me to rest, then shut up." I stared at the growing shadows on my ceiling. "I'm having a conversation with myself. That's—that's just great."

Look, you're not exactly Miss Congeniality, yourself.

"Well, you sound like me, not the Trill. That's a good sign. I hope this is a one-time thing because, you know, listening to a voice in my head is downright freaky-wrong." I also wondered if it was an indication of loneliness or a desperate need for detachment from reality.

You've been under so much stress lately. Go to sleep.

I did. Thank heaven for minivan-sized, fever-reducing gel caps and their mysterious sleep-inducing ingredients.

⚊

MOM WOKE ME up that evening for dinner. I didn't have the appetite, but I definitely had a major temperature going. Half a bowl of chicken noodle soup later, I was back in bed, wondering what death felt like. I hoped Peter would stop by, as I was sure he was out with Trent, looking for the Puppet or even signs of this new fire-wielding girl. I wanted him to see me on the verge of death and realize what he was about to lose, given the recent drama he subjected me to.

Of course, allowing him access to my room proved to be a struggle that night. When Mom checked up on me, she instantly marched up to my open window and closed it.

"Mom, I need the fresh air," I said.

"It's cold tonight."

"I know, but I'd rather breathe in fresh air. It feels good." I peered at her with my best impression of sad puppy eyes. Half the time the effort worked. Apparently, the other half included that moment.

Mom frowned at me, her back against the window. "No. Absolutely not. Besides, what fresh air? This is Vintage City, Eric."

All right, she had a point. "Well, can I breathe in fresh chemically-treated air then?"

"Don't be funny. Go to sleep. I'm calling your school in the morning." Mom appeared to move away from the window but then hesitated. She even crossed her arms over her chest as she leaned against the glass. Damn it. If Peter planned to show up, it was going to be any minute now. "Honey, is there anything going on with you?"

"Me? No, why?" I threw an anxious glance at the darkness outside, my eyes scanning for shadowy movement.

"I don't know. You're acting strange lately."

I swallowed, grateful for the four—or was it five?—layers of blankets that hid all signs of guilt. "I don't know what you're talking about. I've been stressed about school—the usual way."

My words stumbled when I finally spotted movement, quiet and fast, outside my window. There was a soft flash of something, a faint shimmer of gold that marked the progress of something that flew across the window and then vanished in the night.

"Oh, man…"

"What was that?"

"Nothing, Mom. I'm just, you know, not feeling good."

She watched me for a few more agonizing seconds. "Eric, somehow I think that you're hiding something from me."

I retorted, "I'm not. Okay? Can I rest now, please?"

"If there's anything—"

"I know, I know. If something's up, I'll tell you. 'Night, Mom."

She sighed and threw her hands up, but finally abandoned her position by the window and walked to the bed to press a kiss against my forehead. "Good night, honey."

I had to listen for her footsteps to fade down the stairs before dragging myself out of bed and tiptoeing—in a drunken zigzag—to the window. I pushed against the glass panes as they swung outward with a soft squeak.

"Peter?" I called softly, looking left and right for signs of him hiding in the shadows. "My mom's gone. It's safe to come in."

I heard nothing, no answering whisper, no stealthy movements, no breathing, nothing. Frowning, I leaned farther out and looked all over.

"Peter! Where are you?"

Still nothing. Stray voices here and there from the street, an occasional car chugging past, a dog barking from some unknown distance, but no answering call from Peter. I cussed left, right, and sideways under my breath and then closed the window. I was sure I'd seen him outside just a few moments ago. I figured that he caught sight of Mom and decided not to hang around. I didn't blame him. It sure felt like an eternity getting rid of her.

I crawled back into bed after turning off my light. If Peter wanted to talk to me, he had my number. All the same, I couldn't help but feel confused about everything. I was trying hard to make things work between us, wasn't I? Or were my efforts just not enough? Was there something else going on I didn't know anything about? Did I smell?

"If I only knew how to read minds—or read the future—or just have some kind of superpower…" I withered as the words died in my throat. It always came down to superpowers, didn't it? No matter where I looked for answers, there it was, staring me in the face.

Superpowers. In my case, a total lack of.

MY FEVER WAS gone by the following morning, but I was still pretty weak and headache-y, so I stayed home from school. The weirdest thing, though, was that I was beyond exhausted despite my ten hours of sleep. It felt as though I only had a couple.

"You just had a twenty-four hour bug, honey," Mom reassured me over breakfast, which I'd insisted on having downstairs. I couldn't understand why, but I didn't want to be alone in my room. Maybe I had a nightmare that I couldn't remember, and it was totally haunting me psychologically the next day. "It's normal for you to feel as though you just got your blood supply sucked out by a vampire."

"Oh, come on, Mom," Liz protested. "We're eating!"

"Sorry. You know what I mean, though." Mom raised a brow at me as she scooped the last pancake from the griddle and set it atop the steaming pile on the platter she held. "You went through a crisis last night, and it drained you, even while you were asleep."

"Is there scientific proof of that?"

"Liz, I'm talking to your brother."

Liz shrugged and turned her attention back to her cereal while eyeing me with some suspicion.

I figured she thought I was pretending to be dying a slow, awfully dragged-out death just to get out of school that day. She should be grateful I no longer colored my food blue just to gross her out. Of course, if she kept getting on my bad side, I was sure not against going back on my resolution to be more mature.

"Oh, ho!" Dad suddenly cried from behind his paper. The morning paper, this time. "That's one for the good guys!"

"What? What?" Liz prodded, eyes widening. She might not want to admit it, but she was just as big of a fangirl as Bambi Bailey was over our superheroes. I could tell it took everything she had to keep herself from tearing the newspaper from Dad's hands.

"Mannequin Man and his sidekick—"

"Calais," I corrected.

"Yeah, him. They caught a couple of the Puppet's men last night, just as they were about to break into a store. Not a jeweler's this time. I think they robbed all the jewelers in the city by now."

I grimaced when a bowl of hot oatmeal appeared, and the usual welcome scent of cinnamon and apples tickled my nose. Nothing about it appealed to me that morning, though, and when I looked up to protest, Mom's answering glare pretty much shut me up.

"Eat, Eric."

"Okay, okay. Just don't blame me when I puke into everyone's cereal."

Liz scooted her chair closer to Dad. "So are they talking? What happened?"

"Liz, calm down. They got caught. We'll find out more next time." Dad paused. "Well, this I can say, though—those thugs? They're not human. They're literally life-size, moving dolls."

CHAPTER 6

OKAY, ANY QUESTIONS about homework?

"Nope. I got them. Thanks, Althea."

No prob. It was weird not having you in school, though. Peter and I've had more absences than you, now that I think about it.

I grinned. "I know. Bunch of slackers." My mood faded a little. "Is—uh—is Peter still pissed at me?"

Don't think so. He didn't say anything or show anything to suggest that. Why, do you think you pissed him off well and good this time?

"Yeah, like, enough to make him want to break up."

Over a stupid locker?

My face warmed, and I shrugged helplessly. "I know, it's dumb, but he didn't even want to return my calls yesterday. I left him maybe four. And I said I was sorry after school. I don't know what else he wants from me, you know?"

Yeah, I guess he's a bit sensitive.

"A bit? Sure, if your definition of 'a bit' means elephant sized—and I mean elephant with severe elephantiasis everywhere." Which made for a pretty gross mental image, by the way.

Eric, you know him better than I do. Hey, do you want me to be, like, a bridge or something?

My heart dropped. "Althea, don't screw around. I don't want you playing anything when it comes to me and Peter. Let me handle things."

Okay, but my offer still stands. I've never been a go-between for two gay boys before.

"Or any other boys, for that matter."

Oh, you're SO funny.

I tapped my pen against my desk as I stared at my notes. "What's new in the superhero side of things?"

Hmm. Oh, yeah! Check this out. Peter asked me to see if I could tap into those walking dolls that were picked up, but I wasn't able to. I couldn't. It's pretty creepy, Eric. It's like we're looking at old, old technology. Makes me think of Jules Verne type of stuff.

I straightened in my chair, suddenly alert. "No kidding. You're talking about a steampunk kind of thing? Old-time machines and wind-up dolls and all that?"

Exactly! From what Peter's told me, once they figured out how the dolls worked, the machinery just died, and no one knew how to get them back up again. So now they've got a couple of useless dolls in jail cells and no leads.

Man-sized walking dolls in jail cells? That was new. Then again, I really shouldn't be surprised at this point.

"That's bizarre. It almost sounds like their batteries were taken out or something. Or, like, they had an expiration date."

Yeah. But the police department's still working with Trent and Peter, so when we talk about this, something new might have come up.

I must admit I couldn't help but feel a stab of jealousy at the thought that Peter and Althea were kickass crime-fighting buddies, that whatever transpired was firstly theirs to talk about and analyze, and I was kept outside the elite circle of two. Anything I learned about villains and how they worked had largely been handed down scraps of information from Althea, not Peter.

She was willing to talk about it with me, but he continued to hold back as though he didn't trust me at all.

And that bit pretty hard.

Hey, what's up?

"Oh, nothing. Just wishing that I'd hear about this sort of thing from Peter."

I don't know, Eric. He's got his own way of doing things. You gotta give him room for that. I don't mind talking about superhero stuff with you, really.

"I guess I should get used to being involved with a super-hero," I said with a forced little smile. It was time to end the conversation. "He tells me things, yeah, but only if I ask."

Sounds like a guy, all right.

I shrugged.

It'll take a while, I guess. I'm still coping with the fact that I'm not immune to chores, and I'm the damn superhero in the family!

"Reality sucks, doesn't it?" I set my pen down and pushed my chair back. "Okay, I gotta go and take more meds. I guess I'll see you in school tomorrow."

Yeah. See you. I'll let you know if something new comes up. I'm just waiting for Peter to contact me again for more undercover type of work. Man, this is exciting.

The monitor died, and I stood up, feeling more bothered than before. Oh, sure. Peter would contact Althea at the drop of a hat while ignoring all my phone calls. I could see how it was. I stalked out of my room and headed downstairs, grateful everyone had gone to work or school. I needed to be alone for as much of the day as possible. Sulking and self-pity didn't allow any room for company, and I was in the mood for epic levels of wallowing.

School had let out an hour ago, which meant that I only had a couple more hours—maybe three—before my family would be back home. I took my medication and hurried back upstairs, a sudden resolution filling my mind and energizing me even with my weakened condition.

I gave myself a quick sponge bath and dressed up, checking the clock every five minutes to gauge my progress. After brushing my teeth and combing my hair, I shrugged on my winter jacket despite the warm-ish temperatures outside, and left the house with my bike.

I knew where the antique store was, and I headed there without a second thought. I was determined, more than ever, not to return home until I secured a job there, or anywhere, for that matter. Child labor laws and parental permission? I'd have to deal with those later. Besides, leaving the house and doing something for myself distracted me from Peter. Better than epic levels of wallowing, no?

The antique store that Althea had been pimping out to me was a small shop tucked away in a dark corner of Fourth Street. Heavy furniture, faded knickknacks, chipped oil paintings and china—nearly every inch of space in that tiny, murky shop was cluttered with old things that smelled strange and gave me the creeps. I could've sworn I spotted some stuff that must have been on pirate ships, not including a wooden mermaid statue with dirty, cracked paint.

I nearly freaked out when I saw the damn thing peering out at me from one of the darkest areas of the shop.

I swept my gaze across the area when I stepped across the threshold, and that was enough for me to be overcome by the gloomy atmosphere of the place. The store had lights, yeah, but they were on the dim side—like they'd been chosen to add to the overall look of the place or something. I could feel the weight of time pressing down on me, like each piece being sold was totally possessed with it. Years and years' worth of lifetimes and private stories seemed to whisper to me from all corners as I picked and squeezed my way farther and farther inside. Seriously, it was like being in one of Dad's old Vincent Price movies, only without the coolness of Vincent Price anywhere.

Faint music broke up the heavy silence. Classical music. Violin music. I tried to shake off all associations with the Devil's Trill, especially when I thought I recognized the piece that came on.

I remembered hearing it being played in school by one of the music students who stayed late, practicing his lessons.

"That's Beethoven's minuet," Peter had said when I paused

to listen to it. "My mom has that on one of her Beethoven CDs."

I caught a glimpse of the counter and made my way toward it, humming the tune to myself. A woman sat behind the counter, reading a book that seemed to be just as old as everything else in the shop. She looked up and watched me as I neared, giving her a nervous little smile.

"Hi, may I help you?" she asked in a low, raspy voice.

"Hi, how's it going?" I stammered, shoving my hands deep in my pockets. "I was wondering if—if you were hiring right now."

"Full-time or part-time?"

"Um, part-time?"

She set her book down and leaned forward, resting her elbows on the counter and clasping her hands as she stared at me in silence for a short but really awkward moment. Althea had told me the woman reminded her of one of those gypsies from old books and stuff. I wasn't sure how, but then again, I figured my friend was just getting me all turned on by the idea of working for strange people.

The woman in the shop looked to be in her early or mid-thirties. Her hair was full and curly, a nice reddish-brown shade that fell past her shoulders. She was pale, but then again, if she spent most of her hours tucked away in the shop without exposure to light of any kind, it shouldn't come as a surprise. Her eyes were a weird kind of light blue, a pretty creepy color when they fixed their gaze on me. I felt like I was being stared at by a porcelain doll or a glassy-eyed corpse.

Whoa.

Otherwise, though, she looked normal and even modern. Her black turtleneck enhanced her figure just as nicely as her jeans, which were just this side of skintight. I could think of a long list of straight boys from school who'd kill to take her out for a date—if they were her age, that is, unless they were into women who were, like, twice their age. In which case, they were fucking pervs.

"Have you worked retail before?" she asked, and I shook

my head, my confidence withering.

"No. This would be my first job."

"How old are you?"

"Sixteen."

Then came the crazy weird part. For the briefest moment, she looked as though she recognized me, or at least saw something familiar in me.

"You're an Olympia..."

I blinked. "Uh—no, I'm a guy. My name's Eric." I frowned, completely confused now. "Do I look like someone called Olympia?"

Her brows, raised high just a moment ago, now came together in a deep, thoughtful furrow. Those pale, glassy eyes continued to stare long and hard at me, like they were looking for something. For what, I'd no idea. All I knew then was the seriously freaky feeling of being eaten alive by sight. I expected to have nothing left of me by the time she'd done. My shoes, maybe, or a piece of tattered and bloody cloth or even a patch of skin quivering in a pool of gore.

I cleared my throat. My hands were damp inside my pockets. "I just wanted to say that—that I'm a good worker, and I learn pretty fast. I, uh, I'm pretty handy at taking out the garbage. Or washing dishes."

She nodded, pursing her lips and tapping her perfectly manicured fingernails against the countertop. "Hang on a sec. I need to go to the restroom," she said, sliding off her chair and vanishing into a back room. I didn't even see the door. In the dim light, it simply blended into the wall. I took several deep breaths to calm myself, coughing violently when I breathed in dust instead. Jesus.

I BARRELED THROUGH the streets on my bike, glancing at my watch and keeping track of time. My family would be back within the hour. I should be out of my clothes and back in bed before then.

I ran up the stairs and barricaded myself in my room, quickly shedding my clothes and shoving them in a crumpled bundle inside my closet. When I got into bed, I couldn't rest. I stared in disbelief at the ceiling, not exactly sure how I felt. Actually, I was depressed, more so now than before.

The long and short of it was that I didn't get the job. I'd embarrassed myself in the worst way I possibly could—short of walking through the streets naked—and despite Ms. Whitaker being very understanding and sweet, I still left the antique store completely mortified.

Deep down, I suppose, I never expected to get the job. I guess I kind of knew all along it was hopeless for me from the get-go. Save for babysitting, I really wouldn't be able to land something without my parents' signed permission—my home state was being a real big pain in the ass with their laws—and God only knew the nightmares that waited for me in the babysitting business. Children were products of Satan's poop hole, and they'd eat me alive unless I got to them first. Ugh.

So, now what? I was sure, seeing as how I'd survived this long without a job, I'd cope with the disappointment well enough despite the hit my pride took. I was also sure I could make myself useful to my parents in other ways, not just financially. Chores and errands: I could do those. Then again, I'd always been doing those since the moment I'd popped out of Mom, all slimy and gross. It sure didn't look like my sad little existence wasn't going to change anytime soon.

The restlessness that had become so awfully familiar rippled through me again. It felt like a thousand ants marching across my body from head to toe, and I tossed and turned under the sheets, muttering and cursing. It was such a bizarre sensation, and it seemed to grow worse by the day. I couldn't stand it. I couldn't figure out where it came from. The conversation I had with Peter just recently came back, and I toyed with possibilities again.

"I don't know. Even if we weren't going through a financial crisis right now, I think I'd still fight for a job. I just, I feel so restless. All of a sudden, you know? It's been like this for a while now—since—since the Trill got to me. I mean, I wanted to be busier before like, get a job and stuff, but somehow it feels more urgent now."

"You've been through so many tests. Nothing's been found. I doubt if being messed around by the Trill has anything to do with your restlessness."

"I feel like I'm stuffed inside this tiny little box, and I can't move, and everything's beyond my control. Gee, paranoid much?"

"I go through that a lot. Can't say the same about Trent and Althea, though."

"Yeah. Maybe it's something psychological. Maybe I'm jealous that you and Althea are suddenly important heroes, while I'm just this useless average guy with nothing to offer."

Was that the reason? I was growing more convinced it was. I wanted to be useful in one way or another, to my family, to my friends, to the people of Vintage City, not this pathetic doormat with so-so grades. I didn't have the words to show how much that ate away at me. For one crazy moment, I actually wished my parents had had me designed at the genetics lab.

"God, this sucks!"

Time to rest.

"Oh, great, I'm hearing my brain talk again." I sighed. "Am I coming down with something? Am I stressed out to the point of hallucinating? What the hell's up with this?"

You've been through quite a bit of stress.

"Yeah, I suppose I'll get over that. I just don't understand why I'm suddenly so—so dissatisfied and impatient."

You'll understand yourself soon enough.

"I guess so."

Chin up. Besides, you've made some progress here. You earned some downtime.

I made progress? What progress? Embarrassment? Battered pride? I suppose that would be called progress in my case. A weight lifted off my shoulders all of a sudden though I still hadn't been able to answer so many questions about my motivations. I couldn't help but grin stupidly at the ceiling. I was still jobless, I was talking to myself, and it was time for me to move on. Was that good or bad? Too bad I didn't feel sleepy enough for a nap.

What are you talking about? You ARE sleepy.

Oh. I snickered and turned to my side, facing the window and the fading light outside. "Yeah, I guess I am," I whispered, terminating that with a yawn.

My thoughts drifted to Peter as I slowly faded. I'd come home to no messages from him. He must be taking care of homework. Then maybe later he'd be taking a break from cleaning up the streets and spending some time with me like he used to. I frowned against my pillow. I sure hoped he'd gotten over his supersensitivity by this time. I hadn't seen him or heard from him in over a day, and I already missed him like crazy.

CHAPTER 7

"DRAT! FOILED AGAIN! Magnifiman, Calais, Mystery Fire Girl Thwart Puppet's Planned Heists—Three Times!" the newspaper screamed in heavy black and recycled gray the following morning.

"Awesome! Now that's what I'm talking about!" Liz exclaimed, her eyes sparkling as she peered over Dad's shoulder to read the headlines.

Mom marched to the table and set down a steaming platter of sausages next to the plate of rich, greasy tater tots. Just looking at what we had for breakfast was enough for me to feel my arteries constrict again. I almost expected them to sue me for subjecting them to daily mealtime trauma. From somewhere behind me, where the kitchen counter was, came the distinct smell of toasted bread.

My belly gurgled. Now *that* was the breakfast of champions. I shot out of my chair and hurried to the refrigerator, rummaging around for my homemade, natural, sugar-free strawberry jam from Mrs. Horace's kitchen. Carrying my treasure back to the table, I couldn't help but glow with pride at the handmade label, on which Mrs. Horace had nicely scrawled "Eric's Special

Jam." Her homemade jams were to die for, and it had become a bit of a tradition for her to give me a couple of jars whenever she had some leftover after her initial canning process. That was the reason why "Eric's Special Jam" was always half-full or three-quarters full or five-sixths full, never a hundred percent. Whenever I visited Althea on a weekend, there'd be a jar waiting for me. I felt so loved.

When my plate of freshly made toast appeared, I nearly smothered each piece with strawberry jam, vaguely wondering what blue jam would look like. I shook my head. I should ask Mrs. Horace if she made the same stuff in blueberry, preferably denim-hued blueberry.

"It looks like the Shadow Puppet's upping the ante," Dad said as he laid the paper down, spreading it over his plate and silverware. Good thing there was no food on it. He bent over the printed pages, pushing his glasses up his nose as he frowned. "There were at least a dozen of his walking dolls roaming around the streets last night, targeting different stores in the downtown area. In three incidents, the dolls were caught while they were breaking in. The third time around, they barely even made it to the back door when they were—holy smokes!—they were incinerated!"

Dad paused and glanced up, drop-jawed. We all met his look of shock in very much the same way. Anyone who would've walked in on us at that moment might've mistaken us for a bunch of pasty, gross mannequins, wide-eyed with mouths hanging open, breakfast displayed in mid-chew.

"Incinerated?" Mom echoed after a brief silence.

"That's what they say here. There was nothing left of the dolls but wooden legs, still in their pants and shoes, burned and smoking from the knees up. The police say the dolls must've been blasted with fire just as they were walking up to the Aiglentine Perfumery. Around four pairs of legs were found at the scene."

Liz and I exchanged incredulous looks. "Yikes," I breathed.

"It sounds like a cartoon, doesn't it?"

"No kidding," Liz said. "Was it that new fire girl who did it?"

Dad nodded. "Yep."

"So how'd they find out?" I prodded, my curiosity stoked. "If Magnifiman and Calais had their hands full elsewhere, how'd they know where to go to find the third heist?"

"Uh, wait, I'm still reading. Okay, here it is. Apparently the fire girl alerted the police."

"How? Did she torch their car or something?"

"No, no—she—well—she can fly, and she crash-landed on a squad car that was patrolling East 33rd. She hasn't mastered flight yet, they said, and instead of landing on the road in front of the car, she ended up on the hood, pretty much totaled the vehicle. At least she apologized for the damage, according to the police, even offered to help clean up the freeways as part of community service if she had to."

Yes, that definitely sounded like our nervous fire-wielding superhero. "Do they have a description of her?" I asked.

"Other than that she was practically a nervous wreck, not much. Petite, dark hair in a ponytail, black and gold Spandex and a matching mask—she didn't stay long enough for a chat. She flew off and clipped the corner of an old warehouse and caused minor damage there. I wonder if she needs glasses."

I fell silent and wolfed down my breakfast, surprising Mom with requests for seconds. And thirds—Mrs. Horace's jam was an evil influence. While everyone else chatted about the new superhero and supervillain, I mulled things over. Maybe Peter had a chance to meet her last night, even work with her somehow despite all appearances of her working alone. I was sure dying to know more about the new hero on the block.

I also said a quiet prayer on her behalf. It was only a matter of time before Bambi Bailey were to christen her with a name that sounded like something a demon would fart out, unless she'd come forward with her own ID. Seeing as how she was currently having the craziest time coming into her powers, I seriously doubted she had a name on hand right off the bat. I couldn't wait to see the evening news later.

THERE WAS A formerly-long-stemmed rose hidden in my locker—the stem had to be trimmed to fit the cramped space. When I saw it, the universe started all over again. The slate was wiped clean, humanity's sins were all forgiven, the greenhouse effect never happened, and the earth was only two days old. I also melted in a puddle of slightly blue-tinted goo in front of my locker.

Sure, I didn't know how Peter was able to get inside, but he was a superhero, and I'd learned not to question the occasional surprise move from him. He must've figured it all out, maybe with Althea's help, the day I was out sick. Unless, of course, Mr. Dancy had been bribed into a break-in.

With the hallway buzzing with groggy kids fumbling their way from their lockers to their classrooms, I scanned the area for Peter and found him lurking near the end of the hallway, looking a little tentative. I pushed my way through the crowd, the rose tucked inside one of my messenger bag's outer pockets, and nearly tackled him to the ground when I reached him.

"Hey." I grinned, feeling too sappy-goofy for words. "Thanks for the rose."

Peter rubbed the back of his neck, looking sheepish. "It's a delayed apology. I don't think it's enough."

I shrugged, still grinning like an idiot. "It's okay. I mean, I wish you'd returned my calls and all that, but after hearing about what's been going on around the city, I figured you and Trent were too busy. Althea pretty much gave me an idea."

"We were, yeah. I didn't get to your calls till almost midnight, believe it or not. I didn't want to wake you up. I, uh, tried to see you, too, but your mom was in your room. I wanted to go back, but we were swamped with thug activity up and down Vintage."

My eyes widened. "Almost midnight? You and Trent were

out that long? Your mom let you?"

"She did, yeah, but it was urgent business all around. God, that sucked. The Puppet's pretty clever, but I think we're slowly closing in on him. It's not helping Trent's moods, though, and I still have to put up with him."

"I heard you had some unexpected help last night."

"We did, yeah. If you're wondering about the new girl, I can't help you. I don't know anything about her other than what's been said in the news."

I nodded. Silence followed, with both of us squirming in our shoes and looking uncomfortably around, using other students for our shields. I really wished I could hug him right then and there, but it was all I could do to pretend interest in my cuticles.

"Eric, I'm sorry. If you were being a jerk to me that day I screwed up your locker, I was being an asshole back. I just— you're right. I'm too sensitive when it comes to us. Even Althea's starting to get pissed at me."

"Hey, it's cool. Really. I'm just glad it's over."

Peter nodded and took a deep breath. "I, uh, I won't be able to hang out with you for a while," he said, blushing. "Trent and I need to keep working on the Puppet's dolls and find out more about them—and the Puppet as well. We think we're close to discovering his hideout. I'm running back home right after school to take care of homework, and then I'll have to contact Althea. You really ought to check out our doll collection. It's growing pretty fast."

"I understand," I said. That awful feeling of uselessness came back, but I fought against it. "I was going to ask you out to a movie, but I guess I'll go alone."

"I'm sorry, Eric."

I looked around. The hallway's traffic had gone down, and a few stragglers hurried to and fro. All the same, it was still unsafe, so I took hold of Peter's hand and dragged him to the stairwell. He came with a quiet, rueful laugh and didn't put up a struggle. Once we reached the third floor landing, I pushed him against the wall and claimed about a hundred kisses, not giving a rat's ass about the growing bulges in our pants.

He was flushed, his mouth wet and swollen. He stared at me in silence for a bit when I finally broke the kiss—or, rather, impromptu makeout session. "I take it that means I'm forgiven," he stammered.

I gave him my best slutty come-hither smirk and led him out of the stairwell to our first class.

We were the only students left, and we just made the second bell. Althea watched us saunter in, disheveled and flushed, I was sure, and rolled her eyes.

THE MOVIE THING was completely spur-of-the-moment. It was another result of my annoying restless urges, something that came to mind from out of the blue just because I hated the idea of going home after school. With my employment hopes completely obliterated, that mental itchiness seemed to have quadrupled. Quintupled, even. I'd even go as far as it being tupled six times over. Nothing, absolutely nothing, gave me any kind of relief. Books, TV, net-surfing, everything sounded tired and dull.

All of a sudden, the more urgent problem of my family's sucky financial situation had faded to the back of my mind. In fact, I'd practically forgotten about it till that moment when I stood in front of the theatre, fumbling around for my leftover allowance.

"Oh, yeah. We're broke," I muttered, staring at the bills in my fist, feeling nothing about it.

Then I walked up to the ticket booth with an indifferent shrug.

It was a strange moment. Somehow I felt completely detached from my body, as though I were watching myself from outside. An out-of-body experience, some people might say, with all feelings kind of muted, all thoughts limited to nothing else but what I was doing. Purchase ticket. Walk inside. Find a seat. I was aware of the total weirdness of my detachment, but couldn't feel anything significant about it.

The number of people inside seemed no more or no less than normal. I took my usual spot near the back and next to the aisle. When I sat down, I could barely keep still, and it was driving me crazy.

"Oh, man," I muttered, shifting every so many seconds and not finding anything comfortable enough. I thought at first it was just my ass that was being a serious jerk. But it turned out to be much worse than an asshole-y ass. That feeling of a billion ants marching across my body returned, and it was, like, magnified.

"God, what's wrong with me?"

Just let things happen. Let things go. Fighting them won't help you.

I could hear my heart pounding. There was something wrong with me. I knew it for sure no matter how many times I tried to blow things off. The voice I kept hearing in my head was me, and yet it wasn't. I looked around, all desperate in distracting myself by checking out everyone else in the theatre. No dice. The restless stirring increased.

Stop fighting!

"Shut up!"

Stop fighting!

"No! Leave me alone!"

I realized I'd taken my glasses off and pinched my eyes shut the whole time. When I opened them, some of the kids sitting nearby had turned to stare, whispering to each other and giggling when I looked at them. With my glasses in my pocket, people were nothing more than somewhat fuzzy silhouettes, but I could still make out their movements.

"Hey, check this out. He's talking to himself."

"Dude, whatever you smoked, I want some," a girl piped up from somewhere, and a low ripple of laughter swept across the theatre.

"Someone forgot to take his meds today."

I gripped the armrests when the Billion Sucky Ants feeling throbbed till I thought I could hear them scuttling all over me.

The headaches returned as well, pulsing in time with the itchy restlessness.

Let go. Let go. Let go.

"No. I won't. I won't."

You'll crack if you don't. Let...go!

I pinched my eyes shut again and bowed my head, tensing my body against the unbearable sensation that was now spiraling out of control. I felt a few beads of sweat trickle down my forehead, some trailing down my nose before dripping off. My body shuddered under the two fighting forces, and even with the rushing noise of blood pumping through me, I could vaguely hear my seat creaking and groaning from my violent shaking.

"Stop it...stop it...stop it..."

"Hey, you! What're the voices in your head saying?" Another ripple of mocking laughter swept through the theatre. A few kids from somewhere to my left pelted me with crumpled candy wrappers.

A sharp rush of air blew past my clenched teeth, and a force—something like an invisible hand suddenly pushing hard against my chest—threw me back against my seat. I must have let out a cry of pain or terror. I couldn't remember clearly. The world seemed to speed up around me: shapes, colors, all turning into streaks against a brilliant white background. Sounds swelled to a rising wave of painful noise, as though a hundred people were screaming at the same time. My skull nearly exploded.

"Stop! No! No!"

I clawed at something, felt myself sink farther down. I tried to scream as loudly as I could, but something warm and thick swept over me, like an ocean wave, only it felt like solidified air. I blinked and looked up, and everything had turned different shades of red and yellow. I fell back in my seat again as though I'd been punched against the chest. I let out a sound.

Something like a scream—or an ungodly noise that was nowhere near human.

"Hey, what the hell?" someone called out from the end of a

long tunnel. "Shut up back there!"

CALM FINALLY OVERTOOK me. I turned to face the screen, where a number of people were silhouetted against. I saw all kinds of movement in red and yellow. No. I could see details. My glasses were off, and my vision was crystal clear. Where was I again? Oh, yeah, the theatre.

"Get him out of here! He's gonna ruin the show!"

"Yeah, call the management! Kick him out!"

God, how pathetic. There were two—three—figures moving close, all talking at the same time, all spitting out threats. I shook my head.

"Don't even think about it," I said. I sounded so calm, so far away.

In the red and yellow fog of the theatre, I caught sight of hands coming out to grab hold of me. I rose from my seat, the air sweeping me up till I floated, relaxed, a little above ground. It was wonderful, feeling myself cradled by air.

"Hey, weirdo!"

"Psycho!"

"If you're going to freak out, do it somewhere else!"

"Get out of here!"

"Holy shit, is he—floating?"

Tsk, tsk. Idiots. I focused all thought on the theatre, the kids, the seats, the screen. *Go on, morons.* The figures that were approaching me stopped and hesitated. A couple fell back, and I could sense their sudden panic.

Something exploded from me—from my forehead—a burst of warm energy that rippled out and distorted images it touched, sweeping wide in a horizontal flow. It was like a flood of heat waves that pushed and pushed, knocking down and tearing up, letting out a low rumble as it moved. Screams and shouts filled the theatre, people ran or fell, some diving for cover, some getting picked up by the waves and carried to distant parts, to be thrown against walls. Seats literally folded under the force, and some were torn off the floor. The screen wavered then ripped in two.

It was symphonic. Utterly brilliant. I smiled, shuddering in pleasure as I listened—experienced—absorbed. The air that hugged me felt so soothingly warm.

I turned around and walked out, barely feeling the ground against my feet and passing people running toward the theatre I'd just abandoned. Many were shouting or calling out. All of them seemed to ignore me. Once sunlight hit my eyes, the world turned black—for a second or two.

WHEN I OPENED my eyes again, I was standing on the roof of an abandoned warehouse at the opposite end of the city, shivering in the cold.

"What—oh, my God, what happened?" I gasped. I crossed my arms tightly against my chest, but it did nothing against the blasts of arctic winds.

My head was clear and fresh as though I'd just woken up from a good night's sleep. The rest of my body felt tired and sore, though. I glanced down, my heart stopping at the sight of my dirty and torn clothes.

The maestro awaits.

I looked around, but saw no one else on the rooftop—just scattered debris from years of neglect. All the same, someone laughed, a voice carried by the winds from somewhere: soft, gentle, triumphant. Slowly, I grew more and more aware of police sirens wailing from distant parts of the city. I inched forward and peered over the ledge and immediately shrank back. How the hell did I get up here?

CHAPTER 8

THE WAREHOUSE WHERE I was left stranded was only three stories high, thank God, but it didn't make me less freaked over finding a way out. An old door that jutted out on the roof was sealed shut, and no amount of pounding and attacking using filthy junk that looked remotely solid helped. After literally walking the entire perimeter of the roof, I found the fire escape. It was rusty and looked so fragile, but I shook off my nervousness, wiping my nose—because it was now running so badly—against my shirt. I carefully climbed over the ledge and down the rickety ladder.

The final drop to the ground left me half-soaked in stagnant, muddy water because, well, I landed in a puddle of stagnant, muddy water. Just my crappy-ass luck, really. I hurried down one direction, sidestepping more puddles and the rotting debris that seemed to have fused itself to the pavement after sitting there for a gazillion years, and ignoring the occasional homeless person who was curled up under piles of filthy rags or newspapers. Once I reached the first cross-street, I looked around and tried to figure out my location.

The old adult theatre with its dingy, piss-stained walls,

cheeseball posters, and over-the-top neon lights—half of which had burned out—turned into my compass. Ouch. My mom would love to hear that. Cheap, roach-infested sex told me that I was at least twenty blocks away from my house. I was also broke, the only other things on me were my house keys. I didn't have a choice but to walk back, looking as though I'd just been chewed up and then spat out by Godzilla on crack. The entire trek home, I kept my hands shoved in my pockets, or whatever was left of them, seeing as how my jacket hung off my shoulders in tatters, and kept my head ducked. How I managed to reach the front door with nothing to guide me but the sidewalk and my ruined sneakers, I didn't know.

No one was around when I got home, but Liz was due back at any moment. I ran up the stairs and hid myself in my room, jumping inside the shower stall with barely enough time to get all my clothes off. I stared at the sorry pile of dirty and damaged fabric on the floor. The steam thickened around me, and my shivering went away under the soothing warmth of the water.

What the hell was I going to tell my parents? I couldn't remember anything. No, not at that moment, at least. Well, random, broken scenes. Like nightmares, with people screaming and running. Distorted images and lots of red and yellow. And a strange distance—the vague, dream-like feeling of watching everything unfold from behind a TV screen, almost. An out-of-body moment…

What was I doing the whole time? I wasn't sure, but thought I remembered a strange sense of peace in spite of the bizarre nightmare.

"Maybe it'll all come back later," I whispered, my gaze still fixed on my ruined clothes.

Somehow I didn't feel convinced. My legs shook, and I suddenly grew aware of how exhausted and weak I felt. I sank to the floor and sat there, drawing my knees up to my face and staring, confused and frightened, at the water that exploded around me. From a distant part of the house, I thought I heard Liz's voice call out. She came home from school just in time.

My bag had also gone missing. I didn't realize it till way after I stepped out of the shower, refreshed but drained. No wonder that twenty-odd-block walk home didn't turn out as hard as I'd first thought. The usual two-hundred-pound weight strapped to my body wasn't there.

"Oh, crap. Where did I leave it?"

I flopped down on my bed and stared at nothing for several moments, frowning and kicking my brain. I had homework to do, damn it.

"The theatre!"

No way. *No way.* A surge of intense panic overwhelmed me at the thought, and I didn't know why.

All right, well, I suppose it had a lot to do with the fact my last lucid moment was of me sitting down in the theatre. Then something happened, and I still couldn't remember much more than scattered bits that flickered alive for a second and then vanished, to be replaced by more crazy fragmented images and sensations. My next lucid moment was of me discovering I was stranded on some warehouse's rooftop—dumped there and abandoned like that day's trash.

I groaned and buried my face in my hands. "Oh, God, I'm going crazy."

My phone rang, and I jumped. Was it me, or was the sound a little too loud? I got off my bed and hurried to my desk, checking the ringer volume first before answering. It was on low—just as it'd always been.

"Hello?" I rubbed my temples.

"Eric." It was Peter.

"Oh, hey! What's up? I thought you'd be out with Trent by now." I loved the sound of his voice—more so at that moment than at any other. I needed to hear something familiar and normal. I'd rather be with Peter, actually, not talking to him over the phone, but beggars couldn't be choosers.

"I am, actually. I'm sneaking a call to you right now."

"What happened?"

I realized then that Peter sounded pretty serious, more so than usual. "We're at the theatre," he said. I held my breath, my skin prickling. "Something happened here, an explosion of some kind. The theatre—the interior, I mean—it's all torn up."

I swallowed. "What? Was—was anyone hurt?"

"Nothing real serious, thank God. A lot of bruises and sore bodies, but nothing more than that. Most of the damage seems to be limited to objects. The seats and the screen, for instance." He paused. I heard him take a deep breath. "The seats. Eric, half of them were torn off the floor, and the rest were bent, folded. They look like pretzels. I've never seen anything like this before."

"No one died," I whispered, my voice shaking. "That's good."

"No one did, no. I actually thought you were one of the victims."

I swallowed again, bracing myself though I still couldn't understand why I felt this kind of icy fear. "Is that why you called me?"

"Well, yeah. We found your bag in the mess."

"My bag…"

"School bag. Your books and notes and stuff are still inside, but the bag itself looks like it got trampled on by something. I couldn't make out the marks, though. I think, hell, I can't explain it, Eric. When I saw your bag, I just about freaked out and decided to call you the first chance I had." Peter's voice rose and fell like it was reflecting his horror and relief. "I wanted to make sure you didn't get blasted into dust or something by whatever it was that hit the theatre. I was getting ready to claw through the rubble to find you."

I sank to the floor next to my desk. "I'm okay, Peter," I said. "I—I guess I left my bag there. I didn't even realize it till after I got home." I forced out a stiff laugh. "I think I'm getting senile at sixteen."

"I'm so glad to hear your voice." He paused then asked the inevitable. "Eric, do you know anything?"

"I don't, no," I stammered, the words tasting like bile. "I was there, yeah, but whatever happened at the theatre must've taken place after I left. I wasn't feeling too well and decided to ditch the whole thing and go home even before the movie started. I barely made it back, too. Bad headache and queasy stomach. I seriously couldn't think straight." The lie came out so easily, but I needed to cover my tracks, though I didn't know what had happened. Something was taking over—self-preservation at a price—but where did it come from? I had nothing to hide, right? So what was up with the quick, instant, easy lie? I was fast losing control of myself and couldn't do anything about it. "I didn't even realize I'd left my bag behind till after I got out of the shower." That at least was the truth. Not that it balanced anything else I'd said so far.

"You never saw the movie?"

"No." Another sliver of truth there. "It doesn't bother me. It only cost me a buck. What—uh—what are people saying? Has anyone described who was responsible?"

"No one recognized the kid. Yeah, it was some teenager, they said. It's partly because of the dim lights, but they say it's also because the kid changed—shapeshifted—in front of them."

"Transformed, you mean? Into what?"

"Not into a monster or anything," Peter said. "I guess I used the wrong word, but witnesses said the kid acted like he was talking to himself and then turned into this energy-wielding person. They said his skin glowed, his eyes turned white, and he seemed to levitate himself right before he blew the theatre up—smiling the whole time." He took a deep breath. "Details are still pretty sketchy right now. I'm sure you'll find out more when the news comes on tonight."

My heart was beating so violently. It was like it wanted to eat its way out of my chest. I couldn't remember things, and yet I somehow knew I could. I was downright terrified; one part of me didn't know why, while a nagging feeling told me I knew exactly what was going on. It almost seemed as if two people were crammed inside my body, and both were kind of at odds with each other.

"Wish I were there with you," I muttered, hoping he couldn't read through me. I toyed with the phone's cord to calm myself down.

"I'm glad you aren't. It's a mess. The police are here, and Trent's with them right now. I just sneaked away for a bit to call you," Peter said.

"Are you using your cell phone? How are you able to carry it around with you, considering how naked you are with all that tight-ass Spandex?"

"I've got my methods."

Such a tease. I smiled and nodded tiredly. "You'd better get off the phone, you slacker. Some superhero you are."

"Yeah, I know. I just—I love you. I'll swing by tonight with your stuff. Hopefully the cops won't need your books and notes. I'll tell you everything I know when I do."

"Okay. Love you, too. Take care."

He hesitated again. "There's something different about this," he said in a half-whisper—almost as though he were talking to himself. "Something I can't place my finger on."

"Hello? You still there?"

"Oh, sorry. Yeah, I'm getting off for real." Peter chuckled again. "Bye."

I turned around and set the phone back on its cradle. I couldn't do much else other than to stay seated on the floor, staring dully ahead of me. I'd long learned to trust in gut feelings, and what mine told me at that moment wasn't very pleasant.

A nap. Yeah, I supposed I could use one. Sleep was always welcome.

MAYBE I WAS getting better at pretending, but my family suspected nothing wrong that evening. Mom did say I looked sick and pale, and I worked on that suggestion. After dinner, I was ordered to go straight to bed, which I gladly did though I wished I didn't miss the early evening news as a result.

"Hey, that's not fair," Liz cried. "Eric goes to bed early, and I'm stuck with the garbage again! That's two nights in a row! And the dishes—"

"Honey, don't be a drama queen," Mom broke in. "Your brother will make up for lost time when he's feeling better."

Liz pinched her mouth shut, glared at me, but didn't push it. I just went with the flow and ate what I could stomach, not even surprised at my lack of appetite, before abandoning my place at the table and giving Mom and Dad a kiss goodnight.

"I'll check up on you later," Mom called out just as I stepped out into the hallway.

The first thing I saw when I entered my room was the pile of books and notepaper on my bed. Pens, pencils, small sketchbook, and the rose that Peter gave me lay in a neat cluster next to the books. The bag wasn't there. I figured the cops decided to keep it as evidence or something.

"Peter?" I called out, lowering my voice. "You here?"

Silence met me, and I walked over to my bed and looked at my stuff. A small sticky note on my chemistry book caught my eye.

I couldn't stay. I'm sorry. We've got a lead, and we need to get on it before the trail grows cold. I'll talk to you in school tomorrow. Sweet dreams.

I crumpled the note and tossed it away. I was sure a thousand questions just begged to be asked, but I kept them at bay by blanking out my mind. It was oddly easy to do, well, easier than it used to be, anyway. If I were to let just one question nag me, I'd be drowning in a bunch of others that would force their way in, no matter what I did. No—better to stay dull and flat than to grow even crazier from questions I could never answer.

I forced my attention to schoolwork and mechanically went through my books and notes, checking my homework and other things. It was so easy, distracting myself this way. Before I knew it, I was seated at my desk, bent over the review questions for my English class, and scribbling furiously away.

Does he suspect anything? I hope not.

I sighed and shook my head. Without a single break in my rhythm, I continued with my work.

It was a miracle, for sure, because I was done with everything in record time. And I didn't even feel tired from the effort.

I went online the moment I was done. Nothing was posted yet regarding the incident at the Elms Theatre. Then again, which Big Name online news site would want to talk about Vintage City? Nope, I'd have to depend on local online news sites, all of which hadn't posted anything beyond what Peter already told me.

As far as online RPGs went, I was treated to a boom in activity.

Energy Boy was now the new hot ticket, coming close behind Fire Blaster Girl. The Shadow Puppet had been shown the time out corner for apparently creating way too many living dolls that he let loose on the city. All of those things did nothing but commit all kinds of petty crimes that held up the flow of the story—or stories—for too long because other players were forced to fight them off instead of develop the storyline into something existentially meaningful, as one player whined.

I rolled my eyes. "It's a stupid online make-believe game!" I snorted. "What the hell do you expect from it? Philosophy or something?"

Ah, but on another level, it looked like Magnifiman and Bambi Bailey had split up, tearing apart their family. Magnifiman was apparently too caught up with his work to help the missus in raising their children, who now numbered fifteen. With two of them naturally turning into villains, there were four more who were teetering on the edge of badness because, well, Dad and Mom just couldn't get it together. In the meantime, Calais had just proposed to some girl named Anne Fanny-Eliza Dashwood—an unexpected heiress to a great fortune and an estate that made European castles look like goat poo with brightly colored flag-pennant-things. When I checked Anne Fanny-Eliza's player's profile, I found she was "Jane Austen's Number One Fan" and that "All sweet romances are happily ever after. Elizabeth Bennett and Fitzwilliam Darcy for-EVAR! <333"

CHAPTER 9

THE CITY'S OVERRUN by superhumans!" Liz said over break-fast. "How many more are expected to crawl out of the wood-work?" She glanced at me, frowning, and I shrugged.

"They give Vintage some character at least," I offered be-tween mouthfuls of toast and jam. "Otherwise, we're stuck with nothing more than grime, fog, and rain."

Liz snorted. "I'm just waiting for someone to come out with powers that let them animate corpses."

"That'd be cool."

"Figures."

Dad continued to read from the newspaper. It was kind of interesting, I guess, the way his voice worked like wallpaper to my conversation with Liz. Mom had disappeared from the din-ing room when she'd realized her mascara needed some touch-ing up. Maybe the surprise of having genetically-enhanced resi-dents pretty much lost its charm at this point to my sister and my mom, the way things were going.

"Oh, another superhero? Pfft. So what else is new?" was most likely the tone of family conversations all over Vintage

City by now. "Look, another thug from so-and-so's camp was picked up last night. What's the weather going to be like tomorrow? Oh, chemical fog and rain again. Same old, same old."

Same old, same old. The story of my life. Funny how a good night's sleep could change a person's perspective. Yesterday I was in a serious state of shock and panic over the theatre incident, to the point of knowing I was in some way involved in the attack on the Elms Theatre.

Something told me I was in danger from both sides of the law, and I believed it without really understanding why.

I didn't dream last night; my sleep was deep and uninterrupted, and I woke up completely refreshed and even rolling my eyes over yesterday's crazy freak out. Nothing made sense, both yesterday and today, but it was pretty easy to just let things go and accept them without question.

Something told me *that* might have been my hang up the whole time. Maybe. The key to surviving was to be passive and let things happen? It sure looked like it.

"So stupid," I said, laughing, as I stared at myself in the mirror. "You're taking things too seriously—mountain out of a molehill and all that crap. Just let go."

Let go. Yeah, that sounded good.

I suppose the one thing that stood out was the feeling of dissatisfaction that stirred in my chest when I stepped out of the bathroom after washing my face and looked around my room. It was a weird kind of dissatisfaction. It wasn't at all like the epicly annoying rampaging ants type of restlessness that, up until that point, threatened my sanity.

I wasn't sure if I could explain it more clearly if someone were to ask. Maybe the closest I could come up with would be a detached kind of dissatisfaction, like the way one might feel when he was done with something and was on the verge of moving on to the next level. It was like that in-between sort of stage that I felt I was in. What stages would there be, anyway?

Hell if I knew. It was almost as if I'd already accepted that I was done with the past and was ready to turn my back on it and move forward in a new direction.

So, yeah—same old, same old. That was how things were until that moment, and I felt the need for something different without the usual irritations that came with it.

I lost myself in my own little world while voices continued to fill the dining room—Liz's and Dad's, the conversation now shifting to another debate—yawn!—between them. I was pretty relieved when I finished breakfast.

"Okay, I gotta go," I said, standing up after taking a final swig of my milk. "I don't want to be late."

There was a sudden pause in the conversation as Dad and Liz turned to stare at me as though I'd just sprouted another head.

I blinked. "What?" One of my hands automatically flew to my hair. "Is my hair color fading?"

As though on cue, both of them turned to look at the clock. I rolled my eyes and sighed, pushing my chair back.

"Eric, you're forty-five minutes early," Dad said, his brows raised way, way up, as though they were being vacuumed by his hairline.

"That's a record," Liz piped up. "Where's the camera? This needs to be recorded for posterity."

"Yeah, yeah, yeah," I grumbled, marching past them and waving a hand. "So I got up early. Big deal."

I wasn't sure, but I thought Liz mentioned something about pod people, alien abductions and brain experimentations when I stepped out into the hallway. Well, my family was more than welcome to come up with all kinds of conspiracy theories about me, but it wouldn't change the fact that I was gung-ho that morning, and I wanted to get an early start to my day.

Had I been in my old frame of mind, I guess I'd have freaked myself out, too. I mean, forty-five minutes early? What the hell? I'd heard about restless leg syndrome. Was this something like it? It was kind of a creepy thought, someone's legs taking over like that. I wondered if it was caused by one of those hard-to-kill viruses or bacteria that'd be spread around by birds or raccoons or gnats.

PETER CHUCKLED. "OKAY, that's enough. I'm late. Trent's going to be pissed."

"Not that that's going to change anything."

"Eric, you're not at the receiving end of Magnifiman's bitchy moments."

"But we've only been here for, uh…" I stole a glance at my watch. The hands barely glowed in the murkiness of the abandoned classroom. "Three minutes."

Outside, the skies darkened by the second as light showers turned rapidly to buckets and buckets of rain. The lights in the room stayed off, and we were in the shadows. I'd sneaked back inside our English classroom once I'd made sure the upper-floors were empty of students and teachers, and it wouldn't be for another half hour before the janitorial staff began their rounds.

I'd long learned and committed to memory Renaissance High's post-school hours maintenance activities, and for good reason. That moment was the reason, which was a very good one.

I peered through the gloom and watched Peter as he continued to smile at me. "Screw it," I whispered, pressing my forehead against his. "You need a break from all your superhero work. I'm sure your parents will understand."

He shifted under my weight with a groan of pain. I was forced to get off my perch—his lap—to sit beside him instead, leaning against the rear wall of the room, a bit miffed. I watched him rub his thighs as he moved his legs, his body visibly relaxing. We were both sitting on the floor with our legs outstretched. It was my fault, I admit, for sitting on his lap for too long because, yep, I was my usual horny self, and I couldn't stop myself from pawing away at him.

"Thanks," he whispered back. "My legs needed a little more

blood circulating through them."

"Sorry. Hopefully I didn't just screw up your speed ability with my weight."

Peter fell silent as he leaned his head back and turned to regard me. "I don't know how long we'll be working like this, Eric," he said. "I really wish I could take you out or something, do what we used to do before the Puppet came out in full force, but, you know…"

His words faded in the gloom, and I nodded. "I know. I understand. I guess I'm being selfish as usual."

"Is something wrong? Did something happen?"

I frowned at him. "No, why?"

"No, nothing. I just thought I sensed something different about you just now."

"Like how?"

"I don't know. I can sense it, but—hell, I don't know. I think I'm tired. All this running around, chasing after leads that go nowhere, picking up dolls that aren't giving us any help." He exhaled deeply. "It sucks. I hope that new girl steps up and joins us. We need her help."

"She'll probably just destroy Trent's bike or something while trying to land."

Peter laughed quietly. "Maybe. We all need to start somewhere, I guess."

I nodded and turned my attention back to the blackboard across the way. "I'm bored, Peter. I wish I could do something to help you guys, but I know I'll only get in the way. I hate feeling useless when it comes to this. I can see you and Althea working hard together, figuring out what to do next, and all I can do is stay home and do homework." I sighed. "I mean, I'd rather be a supervillain than a boring old nobody."

"Don't say that. You've no idea—"

"I know, I know. I can't help it sometimes." I sighed again. "And, yeah, I know I've whined about this before."

"Keeping yourself safe is the most helpful thing you can do,

Eric. Trust me. Whenever I hear about some incident involving civilians, I automatically wonder if you're there, injured or worse. It's hell." He rested his hand against mine. "I know how restless you get, but I'd rather see you suffer from boredom than be caught in another attack."

"Yeah," I said, my voice fading. "Well, you'd better go, then, before Trent gets completely PMS-y on you."

"Come on," he grunted as he stumbled to his feet. "I'll drive you home."

I wondered if there was a connection between existential restlessness and horniness, I mean, other than the usual teenage hormonal angst crap. I realized I'd grown more and more crazy lusty when it came to Peter, and I'd be, like, jumping him the first chance we got at a private moment. It didn't matter where we happened to be. I'd see him, and BAM! He'd be under attack, and it didn't involve devious sidekicks or hypnotic music or tainted sardines. Only me, trying to get inside his pants despite our agreement that we weren't ready for anything seriously physical. Actually, that'd be more like Peter's agreement and not mine. I kind of just let it go in one ear and out the other. I mean, Jesus, I was sixteen. Sex was the only thing that made sense to me.

That day, I'd gotten my paws all over him—let me see—before our first class, during lunch—now *that* was tricky to pull off, but I managed somehow—after our final class, and in his car when he dropped me off at home. One minute he was talking about homework or having lunch with me and Althea the next day. The next minute I was latched onto him, lost in Olympic-level tonsil-sucking gymnastics while he flailed his arms. I cussed at how we were the same height and that I couldn't squeeze myself between him and the steering wheel for that kiss.

"Bye." I smiled against his mouth, feeling a weird kind of pleasure in seeing him stare at me all confused and shocked. And when I say "weird," I don't mean "kinky." "See you tomorrow."

"Uh—yeah—bye. Wow."

I hopped out of the car, feeling light on my feet and totally unfazed by the barrels of rain that fell on me. I walked—nope, didn't run—to the front door, my keys in hand, turning once to wave goodbye to a still stunned, red-faced Peter. When I walked inside, I felt so energized and cheerful as though my earlier frustrations at getting tangled up with Peter on the floor of our classroom never happened.

I dripped my way up the stairs and to my room, humming to myself. It was strange, but I never felt cold even with my soaked clothes. I just undressed and jumped into the shower, still humming.

Had I been my old self, I'd have creeped myself out. Totally.

I kept to my room till dinner, making sure to get all my homework done before. Then came chores, and it was back to my room, where I barricaded myself. The computer stayed off, and my books were ignored. Once locked away and safe from my family, I threw my window open even though the rain was still going. I watched the night, inhaling the familiar scents of a soaked Vintage City, which could be summed up as Eau de Wet Urban Grime. Someone ought to package the smell and sell it as an effective bug repellant. Or the most effective way of ending a bad date early.

Even with the clouds hiding the moon, I could still make out the jagged outlines of distant buildings, the light from hundreds of windows twinkling, almost.

Your maestro awaits.

I couldn't help but smile. I felt so calm and so content. At the same time, a soft stirring in my belly told me to wait. For what, I didn't know, but I was sure it was a good thing. I suppose that was where my earlier restlessness came from—some kind of gut feeling that encouraged me even if I didn't know why. Then again, I reminded myself it was better to sit back and just allow myself to ride the waves. Sometimes giving up control could very well be the cure to one's spiritual sickness. Or whatever.

Yeah, the peace that came with that idea seemed to grow. I

walked back to my bed and flopped down, curling on my side and taking care to face the open window as I waited. I could see stray raindrops getting blown by the winds into my room. I watched small wet spots form on the floorboards. Mom was going to kill me if she saw that I was letting this happen, but I didn't care.

The rain and the slight chill of the night winds lulled me to sleep, the last thing on my mind before I drifted off being Peter. Naturally.

"ERIC! WAKE UP!"

I gasped just as I felt a rough shaking and a tight ring of arms around my shoulders. I opened my eyes and blinked away the fog.

"Eric! Eric! " Dad said again and again. He held me against him in a firm and uncomfortable embrace, and when I'd fully awakened, I saw I was standing at the top of the stairs. At the bottom stood Mom and Liz, both of whom stared at me in shock.

"Wha—Dad? What happened?" I stammered, sagging against him.

"What happened? You sleepwalked, that's what happened," Dad said, frowning. "If I weren't on my way upstairs, you'd have fallen down the steps and broken your neck!"

I swallowed, completely horrified and dizzy. "How weird," I said as I pulled away from him. "I—I've never sleepwalked before."

Everyone started talking at once: about calling the doctor, having me x-rayed again, maybe seeing a psychiatrist. I barely heard what they all said, but I didn't care. Though still horrified by that close call, I was also amazed at how easily that lie about not sleepwalking before slipped out of me. Not once did I feel bad, and the calm—that incredible feeling of peace and independence—kept its hold. In the middle of the confusion and anxiety over me, I had to turn my eyes and shuddered.

Within minutes, I had more minivan-on-steroids-sized pills

sloshing around in my belly—as per Mom's orders—and I was back in bed, my door shut and possibly secured from the outside with something. Mom also made sure to close my window. If given the chance, she'd have tied me down to my bed to ensure a safe night's sleep. I felt like a gothic heroine.

I WAS BACK in that creepy maze of corridors, all lit up with candles.

"Where are you?" I called out as I turned endless corners.

I still couldn't hear the voice, but I could sense it, and the feeling was much, much stronger this time around. Follow the music, it kept telling me. So I did. Turn after turn, I moved forward, the scent of burning wax and old paint filling my nostrils, the distant sounds of a strange waltz guiding my steps. The music grew louder and louder as my steps quickened.

"Finally!" I cried when I spotted the open door at the end of the corridor. I tried to steal a glance at my watch and saw that I was in costume, something with funky sleeves with those huge, flared, turned up cuffs and white lace ruffles poking out from inside—my shirt sleeve, I thought. I looked down and saw buckled shoes on my feet. Once I understood I was in costume, I began to feel stiff and hot from under all those layers of clothes. My scalp started to itch. When I tried to scratch it, I felt a stiff wig perched on my head.

"You know, this would really suck if I look like George Washington," I grumbled.

Everything smelled so old.

I finally reached the door and walked inside the ballroom, where the party still went on. Lots of drinking, talking, dancing, laughing—people in elaborate costumes packed the room, and I was amazed many of them still managed to dance.

Home at last, the voice crowed.

People who stood nearest to the door turned to look at me

when I walked in. I froze and stared back. Their costumes—I recognized them easily enough. They were in bodysuits of giant orange and black polka dots. They wore wigs that looked like black and orange straw. Their masks were white full types with round eyeholes and bulbous noses and no mouths. If they spoke, I was sure their words would be muffled.

In the background, the strange waltz rose a little in volume, and I recognized the creepy off-key quality of the Solstice Masque carnival. Fear crept up and slowly took over my relief and curiosity. I stood by the door, watching and wondering, while the carnival's costumed workers celebrated with dancing and oddly-tuned music. Some ignored me, and some saluted me with a glass of wine raised in my direction.

I glanced over my shoulder and saw the candles that lined the corridors sputtering and dying one after another, from the opposite end all the way to the ballroom's entrance. It was like an invisible hand was snuffing out each flame between its fingers, and it was working pretty fast. The darkness that slithered forward, following each pair of dying candles, looked like a fast-crawling shadow, hell-bent on catching me.

I stepped closer to the crowd instinctively just as the last candles flickered and died till nothing met my gaze beyond the open door but black emptiness. It was like being in one of those spooky sci-fi movies where people would be trapped inside a room that was caught in the middle of dark, empty space with no way out. Around me the carnival workers swarmed as though nothing had just happened.

Home at last.

CHAPTER 10

"I'M PROBABLY GOING to see a shrink."

"I believe that."

"Shut up, Althea."

"Okay, I guess I can always lie."

I exhaled loudly and threw my companion a vicious sidelong look. "You go beyond suckage."

Althea met my scowl with a proud grin. "I'll wear that like a badge of honor," she drawled. Then she gave me a rough nudge with her elbow. "Lighten up, Plath. I'll bet you they won't see anything wrong with you, and they'll dump you back on your parents' lap."

"I don't think it's that easy," I said, turning my gaze back to the sidewalk and the swarms of people that sucked us both into the same old, same old, late morning current. "I've never been to see a shrink before, so I don't know what to expect other than the couch." I scratched my head and made a face. "And something about cigars."

It was Saturday morning, an abnormally bright and warm day for Vintage City, especially one that came so quickly after the crazy-ass rain of the day before. I'd pretty much given up on understanding how the weather worked in our crummy corner of the world other than that anything weird could easily be blamed on industrial pollution. Peter was again out with Trent, his superhero work hours now reaching totally psychotic proportions. He'd begun grumbling about demanding overtime compensation whenever I asked how things were at the office.

Althea, after a week's worth of hard superhero work giving the good guys nothing but dead ends—the Shadow Puppet was proving to be a bigger badass in the world of supervillains by taking the steampunk route, keeping Spirit Wire from tapping into his toys—took the weekend off with Peter and Trent's blessing. We were now wandering around the downtown area, window-shopping and plain chilling.

She stopped in front of a game store and ogled the new super-violent games it was pimping out to kids. I could swear that I heard her eyeballs pop in their sockets as she pressed her face against the display window.

"Althea, you really are your superpowers." I sighed as I stood beside her. Mutants, zombies, aliens, genetically-altered soldiers, uber-carjackers, prostitutes, monsters—every possible character in a thirteen-year-old boy's wet dreams was there in glorious CG, blood-and-gore-spattered, glaring and snarling at the wide-eyed customer, super-tricked out weaponry in hand.

I heard Althea let out a soft "Oooooohhhh…"

"Girl, there's a growing puddle of drool at your feet."

"I want one of those," she breathed, pointing to just about everything that was on display.

"What for?" I demanded. "You can easily hack into some major MMORPG, create your own character, and kick everyone's asses from now till Sunday and back. You don't need to pay for crap like this."

She pulled away reluctantly, but that was only because I grabbed hold of her collar and physically hauled her off. "Listen, you mobster," she retorted, squirming in my hold and staring daggers at me, "I might have major technology powers, but I don't use them for illegal stuff."

"So what're you gonna do with those stupid games? Super-hero workouts?"

"I don't have to dignify that with a response," she huffed, crossing her arms over her chest and fighting hard to look intimidating, I was sure. Totally made of fail, really, seeing as how she practically dangled from my fist.

"We were talking about my seeing a psychiatrist, Borg Queen," I said, finally letting her go—or more like drop.

She muttered something while adjusting her sweater and shirt. "Look, I told you, take things one day at a time," she replied. We began to move forward, and I begged the cosmos that we wouldn't be passing another game store anytime soon. "Both of us know zilch about psychiatrists, so we don't really know where to start. I mean…"

Althea fumbled for words, before shrugging. "Sorry, Eric. I know it sucks and all, but I've never been in this situation before. Hell, I've never had a friend or family member go through something like this."

"Well—I guess it'll all depend on what Dad and Mom end up deciding on. They talked to me about it, but they haven't made a choice yet. I think they're both against it, but I know that Mom's pretty scared."

Althea nodded and gave me another rough nudge. "I would be, too, if my kid started sleepwalking."

"I've done a little bit of research but really couldn't find anything other than what I suspected and already know. I guess I'm just going through major stress or something. I don't get it. I'm too young for epic levels of stress, aren't I?"

"Well, I should take care of you then, poor baby," she cooed, looping her arm around mine. "I know you and Peter haven't been hanging out a lot, so I'm sure he'll want me to look after you. I'll earn brownie points that way."

"Hey, I'm not a baby."

"Yeah, but he's your boyfriend. Of course he'd kill me if he knew I just let you deteriorate psychologically because, well, you're forced to be celibate."

I was sure I blushed a deep, deep red. I bowed my head to stare at my shoes, embarrassed. "You're really something else, Althea."

"I know. Mom always says that before she grounds me. Here, let's have pizza. That new place, Elephant Pizza, serves huge-ass slices for two bucks. I can afford a feminist date with a gay boy over there." She paused and then added, "They even have a framed shrine to Cher—like, this big box frame with concert tickets and glitter and bits of junk that they managed to tear off her costumes somehow. Dude, you'll love it."

I rolled my eyes.

ALTHEA AND I were nearly dead from grease overload by the time we stepped back out into the sun. On our way out, we passed a huge mirror, and I saw how we looked after our Feminist Date with a Gay Boy. We looked pretty gross.

We could barely walk, and we could barely talk. It was more like a blind stagger and an exchange of grunts and burps as we made our way through the crowds of shoppers. Eventually we just gave up on conversation and simply tried to walk off our fat-saturated lunch. I didn't have any words for how disgusting we both were.

It was somewhere near the main square when everyone, and I mean everyone, stopped in their tracks and looked up. Some people shouted and pointed up. Some screamed. Others hooted and cheered.

Magnifiman flew above us, stunning and heroic even at a distance, with a faint whoosh as he plowed through Vintage City's industrial air, his arms outstretched, his features hard and determined. Beside him, Peter—Calais—bounded, looking strong and graceful as he spanned huge distances with his powerful leaps. He'd fly sometimes, but I figured leaping massive distances worked better for his superpowers. I frankly had zero idea how the hell that worked, but that was the only thing I could come up with. Whatever. Pride swelled in my chest at the sight, and I couldn't tear my eyes off him.

"Something's up," Althea noted, a tremor of excitement in her voice. She fumbled through her bag for her tricked-out cell phone, which was the communication device she always used for superhero purposes. She refused to tell me where she'd got it, but I suspected she and Peter had worked together on it. "Damn, I hope I didn't miss a call from Peter."

"Hey, look!" I said as I grabbed her shoulder.

"What?"

I pointed at the sky. Several seconds behind Peter, a third figure flew, obviously following them. It was the fire girl, and she was flying without a hitch. She wasn't literally on fire, but she did leave a thin trail of flames in the air behind her. They'd probably flicker for a second or two before fading away, but they looked pretty impressive all the same.

"They finally hooked up with her!" I cried, thrilled.

"Uh, I don't think so," Althea said. "Looks like she's trying to run—or fly—after them."

"Oh. Well, I guess it's good that she finally mastered flight."

The girl flew in a confident line across our line of vision, adjusting her course slightly when she neared the old clock-tower—one of the few authentically dated buildings in the city. She swerved up and above it, clearing it just nicely. It wasn't till a moment or so after she'd disappeared from view I realized I'd been holding my breath the whole time, waiting for a disaster to happen in her wake.

"Yeah, looks like she did," Althea said. "Good for her."

Sure enough, from somewhere in the rooftops, a distant, high-pitched yelp broke through the air, followed by the sound of something metallic and old getting knocked over. It was like a pile of old tin platters getting dropped on the floor.

Althea grimaced when sounds of the mishap gradually faded. "Okay, then. I guess not."

"I wonder how it'd look once all the superheroes come into their powers. When they all fly or leap like that as a unit. I think they'll look amazing, just awesome." My chest tightened at the thought. I fought off the jealous pang and tried to focus more on Peter and how lucky I was to be with someone as fantastic as him.

Several moments after the trio had vanished past the rooftops, excited shoppers chattered while going back to what they were doing. Althea turned her attention to her cell phone and frowned. Then she shook her head as she snapped it close and buried it back inside her bag.

"Nope, nothing," she said. "Whatever's up, it happened only now. My communicator's on standby just in case."

"Maybe—"

Althea let out a little screech of delight when her bag suddenly gave off a muffled buzz.

"Action! Yes!" She dug her hand back inside and pulled out her communicator, flipping it open and staring, wide-eyed and practically salivating, at the tiny screen. "Gotcha. Hey, listen, Eric, I gotta go. The Puppet's on the loose, in broad daylight this time, and—"

A low boom cut through the downtown area, bringing conversation and movement to an immediate stop. People looked around and even above them, baffled.

"Damn it," Althea breathed, then pushed her way through the crowd, craning her neck as she scanned the area for only God knew what. I followed her before she vanished from sight.

"Wait!" I called out, but she didn't seem to hear me.

We wove our way through the busy sidewalk, ignoring another low boom that broke through the growing confusion. That time, I felt the ground shake. So did everyone else, for that matter, and people cried out in alarm. Some froze where they stood, and others scattered, searching for cover. All around, people ran inside shops for safety. Traffic slowed, with some cars and cabs coming to a standstill. Within seconds frantic shouts mingled with car horns.

"Althea, where are you going?" I called out.

"Leave me alone!" she retorted as she expertly dodged frantic shoppers. "Get out of the way, Eric! I've got something to do!"

She pushed her way to an ATM and immediately "accessed" it by pressing her hand on the keypad, her fingers splayed, her face hardening as she connected, or her mind connected, with the system. Behind her people continued to hurry in their panic, while another low boom rent the air.

This time it was louder, and the ground moved under my feet. I staggered back a couple of steps with a gasp of surprise. I saw a few people—mostly seniors—lose their balance from the tremor and topple over, nearly getting stepped on by frightened passersby. Thankfully there were some people who jumped in to help them.

I glanced back at Althea. The keyboard under her hand glowed faintly, a far cry from the first time I saw her access an ATM. Maybe this was a sign she had much better control of her powers now. She looked no more like a statue to me, standing before the machine that way, completely oblivious to what was happening around us.

"Girl, what're you doing?" I hissed. "You're blowing your cover! Get yourself to a private computer or something!"

When she didn't respond, I took on the role of her side-kick, standing close and keeping an eye on people. Pretty much making sure no one saw her doing what she should be doing behind closed doors. To my relief, the entire downtown area was too busy being in a state of panic that everyone ignored two pizza-filled kids standing still and off to the side as people stampeded around them. I balled my hands into fists just in case, ready to jump anyone who'd try to get at Althea.

"Shit!" she cried all of a sudden. "Damn it!" She pulled her hand away from the keypad as though she'd just been burned. She staggered back a step or two, eyes wide and blank.

Althea blinked rapidly several times, and the look of shock on her face gave way to anger. She cussed up a storm again, and without another word, pushed me aside and ran back through the crowd.

I could only guess she was hurrying to get back home, where she could safely access her computer and be better connected to whatever it was she was trying to link herself to.

Like what she should've done in the first place. Sheesh.

Police sirens broke through the noise, the shrill wailing growing ever stronger…

…BUT THE CALM proved to be far more intense. I felt protected, enveloped in peace and contentment, despite the escalating excitement around me. I turned to watch three squad cars force their way through traffic, which was now nearly at a complete stop.

I snickered. "How pathetic."

The world had turned red and yellow.

I looked back at the squad cars, which now had traffic in a hopeless jam. Cars inched this way and that, moving in odd diagonals just to get out of the police's way, only to stop dead when they hit the curb. Some of them narrowly missed running over pedestrians.

The noise, the confusion, the panic—I took a deep breath and absorbed everything. I felt my chest expand and my spirits become energized. I looked at the sun and smiled at the vast red and yellow sky, pulling my glasses off because they were blurring my vision, not helping it.

Symphonic. Perfect discordance.

Someone screamed all of a sudden. Then a few more voices joined the chorus. I turned to find several people running out of a side street crammed with small boutiques, some of them looking back over their shoulders to what was chasing them.

"They're coming! They're coming!"

Traffic died. A couple of people scrambled out of their cars and took off running. Others seemed frozen in terror at the wheel. Police officers, blocked from their purpose, jumped out of their cars with their weapons drawn and ran in the direction of the rapidly emptying side street.

Do it!

I hurried away, still lost in that strange calm despite the confusion around me. I ran around cars, pushed my way past frightened people, and hurried to the founder's statue, climbing up and taking my position next to the vandalized figure. Below me, the streets swarmed with frantic activity. If anyone noticed me up there, surveying everything, no one yelled at me to come back down and find shelter.

Shelter? What a stupid idea.

Do it!

From somewhere inside me, somewhere deep in my mind, a small, light voice called out. It sounded like me, but younger. Much, much younger and so far away. Pleading, frightened, and fading quickly. I could actually hear it as it fought for attention in my head.

No, don't! Eric, wake up! Don't listen to him! He's screwing with your head again! Please listen to me! Don't shut me out!

Heat throbbed in my head, a familiar warmth that bordered on uncomfortable and amazing.

Eric, no! Listen to me…

"Listen to whom? Why should I?" I breathed, smiling at the scene.

It's me! Wait!

"Go to sleep."

Wait…

From the side street, a number of strange-looking men tottered out. There were about a dozen of them, all dressed in Zoot suits, all wood grain-faced with no features, all moving in spasms and jerks as though an invisible puppeteer were tugging at their strings. I narrowed my eyes and took a better look. My vision had improved, gone beyond normal. The faceless, tottering men were armed with guns, the old kind, like the ones I'd seen in those black-and-white vintage gangster films. What were they called? Tommy guns or something?

They didn't aim. They just held those guns at waist-height and began shooting, spraying the area with bullets, while people screamed and ran for cover. Here and there, car windows shattered from the assault. Passengers and drivers who hadn't abandon their vehicles vanished from view. Whether or not they were struck by bullets, I couldn't tell. I saw no blood anywhere, though, which made me wonder what was in those guns to begin with.

The police began to fire back, using cars for their shields. A few man-sized dolls staggered, clothes tearing under bullets, but they held up and continued to move jerkily forward, still firing their guns.

Do it!

The heat pulsed, my head completely enveloped now. With a low cry, I let loose a wave of warm energy, watching it sweep across the street in a flood that distorted images. It knocked people down, dented car roofs, and eventually swept around police officers, picking them up and carrying them off, shouting and dropping their weapons. They were transported far, far down the street, to wherever the energy wave died, I suppose. That panicked, fading voice—my conscience?—was now quiet. I liked to think it was gone for good. Or at the very least forced into sleep. I sure didn't need to be slowed down by stupid, whiny protests.

The doll-men were now free. I'd just given them a hand.

CHAPTER 11

EVERYTHING HAPPENED SO quickly in a blur of color, light, sound, and mayhem. It was simply beautiful. I kept my place on the founder's statue, holding back and observing. I'd much to learn, maestro told me from somewhere in the murky past—or maybe my dreams? Watch and wait.

Watch and wait.

The doll-men inched forward. They were running out of ammunition now, but they continued to hold their guns, moving them side to side as though still shooting an endless rain at the crowd. Instead, I only heard an erratic Pop! Pop! Pop! as their weapons emptied themselves.

Some people trapped in their cars screamed as the dolls neared; others managed to stumble out and crawl between cars in hopes of dodging bullets, or whatever those mannequins used against them.

From somewhere to my left—the rooftops, to be precise—a dark blur tore through the air, leaped down onto the mess of cars, and landed right in front of the advancing group. He stood up quickly, his red-brown and gold costume distinctive even in the confusion.

I watched Calais fight, wonder and something much deeper stirring in my belly at the sight of this young, agile hero throwing himself without a moment's hesitation into an old-fashioned fistfight with one mannequin after another. At times, he became no more than a blob of color—no doubt because he moved at super speed to dodge blows—and sometimes he appeared somewhere above or behind an enemy, swinging an arm to deal a massive blow against the back of a wooden neck or the side of a wooden head. He'd use his legs and booted feet to fell a mannequin-doll or two. His moves were very eastern, I thought. Martial arts, that is, and coupled with his incredible speed, he appeared to be a beautiful work of destructive art.

The dolls proved to be much more difficult to bring down, though. Calais would knock them off their feet, but they'd struggle back up, lunging at him with renewed energy despite their increasingly erratic movements. Their guns were useless at this point. They'd run out of ammunition, and Calais had managed to disarm half of them.

Calais was alone at first, moving back and forth, taking on however many enemies would jump on him. From a good enough distance, I could see exhaustion setting in. He gritted his teeth, his breathing growing more pronounced till he was visibly panting from his efforts. Not once did he give up, though, and when caught off-guard and thrown off his feet, he bounced back.

"Hold on!" someone cried.

My breath caught. I heard the voice, and it came from a pretty good distance. First, my eyesight, now my hearing. A thrill swept through me at the possibility of other enhanced senses.

The fire girl now came swooping down from somewhere. She landed, miraculously unharmed and on concrete, not on a car, several feet behind Calais.

"Quick! Take them down!" Calais huffed as he kicked one doll's back, sending it sprawling on the ground. He dove and grabbed hold of its head, yanking it off its joint. The sound of splintering wood reached my ears. The mannequin-doll-thing collapsed in a broken heap under his weight.

"Got it!"

Fire Girl stretched an arm out to her side, and from her gloved hand—the palm, as a matter of fact—something long, slender, and edged with flames emerged. Like a fiery tentacle, it sprouted from her hand and pushed outward, growing till she stopped it by wrapping her fingers around what could be its handle. She stood with a long whip in her hand, which she immediately snapped back as she flew up and above the group of half-broken mannequins.

"Watch it, Calais!" she called out. Calais understood. Wrenching one more wooden head off its battered shoulders, he leaped out of the girl's way just as she cracked her flame-edged whip.

With deadly accuracy, the whip sliced across the group of wooden dolls, decapitating those it managed to reach, sending their headless bodies crumpling to the ground in a heap of burning wood and cloth.

"Excellent!" Calais whooped. He immediately threw himself against a couple of dolls that had managed to escape the fire whip. All three went down in a tangle of bizarre, costumed limbs.

Fire Girl turned her attention to a couple of dolls that had turned tail and were beginning to totter off in a clumsy retreat. She snapped her whip back, the flames crackling up and down its slender, slithering length.

Now. Now!

I felt the energy stir and throb in a fraction of a second. Suddenly I was airborne—or at least I felt weightless—and I kept my mind on the scene before me. Clenching my fists at my sides, I hurled out another wave of energy, this time aiming for Fire Girl just as she was about to crack her whip against the two retreating dolls.

The waves rippled across the air and caught her in mid-flight, cocooning her in suffocating warmth. She dropped her fire whip and flailed in the cloud of energy that engulfed her, her mouth wide open as she struggled for breath. She stayed suspended in the air for a second, struggling and gasping. Below her, the two battered dolls fell under Calais's blows.

He stopped to look up.

Run!

Our gazes met. I killed my energy surge, and Fire Girl tumbled down with a cry and landed on a car. She lay there, stunned and breathing heavily, but looking otherwise unharmed.

I caught the split second when Calais prepared to launch himself after me. I immediately poured out another energy wave in his direction, catching him in mid-leap this time, knocking him off his center and sweeping him away. Like Fire Girl, he flailed against the warm energy that encased him. I turned and flew off, my breath catching in my throat as I sailed in a wide arc above rooftops toward a random spot in the projects.

That was close.

I chuckled just as I landed on a rusty, rickety old fire escape. It faced a grimy old alley, and I had to turn away in disgust at the stench—so common in these miserable places. Calais was going to come after me, I reminded myself. I turned to the filthy window that led to the fire escape. It was partially open, and I gingerly pushed it up, crawling inside with some effort when the damn thing got stuck midway. Once inside, I turned and pulled it back down before melting into the shadows of the room in case Calais or Magnifiman or Fire Girl came my way.

I looked around and found myself in an empty room, neglected and well on its way to being condemned, I was sure. Paint peeled off walls and the ceiling in large patches, exposing plaster or rotting wood. There were a couple of dilapidated chairs nearby, both of which were faded and torn. I was sure all kinds of bugs or rodents must have taken up residence among their rusty springs. The floor was littered with debris from heaven knew where. From somewhere a steady rhythm of dripping water could be heard.

I took a calming breath as I leaned against a wall, enclosing myself in the darkness. I tried to wrap my mind around what had just happened, but I couldn't. Everything had happened at such a rapid rate that even in the peace and quiet of a forgotten home, I still felt outside myself, floating in space, completely in the mercy of something far, far greater than I. I'd no control over anything. Not even myself.

That's where power comes from. Give up all control, and you'll rise above the common and the dull. Do you realize you're now one of THEM?

"I am, aren't I?" I breathed, wide-eyed and amazed.

You are. Are you enjoying it?

I mulled things over for a brief moment. "I am. It's exciting. I can help or destroy at will."

At will? Are you sure about that?

"Well, I'm still learning, aren't I? I guess this is what they mean when they say 'coming into his powers.' I'll have to depend on you for now till I'm able to stand on my own."

That's a charming thought. Do you regret anything?

"Should I?" I laughed quietly in the filthy gloom. "No, of course not. This is a great sandbox I'm in."

Then go explore. It's your time now.

A sudden noise outside silenced my mind. I held my breath as I pushed back against the wall. Voices, low and conversational, male and female. I was sure those were Calais and his new crime-fighting buddy. Could Calais hear me breathe, given his super hearing? My heart pounded; could he hear that as well? I dared not sneak a peek and simply waited. The voices grew a little louder, and before long, I could hear footsteps on rusty, decaying steel. They were moving up and down the fire escape, most likely looking through windows and investigating empty rooms. My hearing, just like my eyesight, had improved tremendously since my powers had taken over, but I knew my ability to hear beyond a certain distance was nowhere near Calais's.

They were now downstairs, in the empty apartment one

floor below me. I could hear them picking their way through the debris, their voices a constant, low hum. If I moved to go to the main door and escape to a different empty apartment, Calais would know.

You can levitate.

All right, then. Never mind.

Concentration was all it took. I raised myself off the floor and focused on reaching the door. It was old and decrepit, just like everything else in the room, and was likely to make all kinds of loud, obnoxious sounds when moved.

Use your powers on it. Seal it in a vacuum the way you sealed Calais and the girl.

I did. It took a little more effort controlling the flow of energy as it rippled out of me, being so used to working with it in larger, more dramatic amounts. A couple of attempts were needed, and I made a mental note to practice some more.

I watched the door shiver and contort as a mass of energy encased it.

"Upstairs. I think I heard something," the male voice said. Then I heard movement—stealthy shuffling through dirt and debris, followed by the cautious rattling of rusty steel as the two superheroes clambered up the fire escape to the floor I was on.

Damn it. I turned the knob and slipped out the door, quietly, effortlessly. It was great. I'd cut off the energy surge just as the sounds of voices and footsteps filled the vacant room at the other side of the door.

Get out.

I did. Still levitating, I floated—no, I could fly now!—toward a window that was way at the end of the dark, rotting corridor. I shot out and flew off to another direction, stopping and hiding behind warehouses and tenements to make sure I wasn't being followed. Every so often, I'd leap down to some dingy alley and crouch beside a dumpster to limit my presence above. God, the stench! My stomach turned, but I stuck to my task, feeling more and more confident with every danger-filled moment of playing hide-and-seek with some pretty powerful superheroes. I was only now coming into my power, and yet I'd been able to avoid them. This was fantastic.

The voice suggested going to a place where I was least likely to be followed. I smiled to myself. Yes, I never even thought about that. Mentors were good to have around. Once sure of my safety, I continued my trek across the city, above and below, with plenty of pauses along the way for security's sake. The delay in getting to my intended destination was a bit of a pain, but as long as I got there in one piece, that was all that mattered.

Good job. A little slow, but you'll improve in time.

I BLINKED AND held my breath. I felt like myself again and yet not. I was back in my own body, so to speak, but everything seemed off. For one thing, I found I was flying and descending to a rooftop. My brain was totally clear, but I was too stunned to freak out over my tweaked self. Yeah, I was tweaked—really tweaked. It was like having two personalities merging into one. The last several moments, it felt as though another part of me needed to take over first, fighting the heroes and then saving my skin, before helping my real self ease into place. Into my new body. And yet that other self stayed in the background, in a way, because I felt as though it'd never left. Like it was watching me from the sidelines, coaching me here and there the whole time. And that other self felt older somehow. An older me, hanging around and sharing mental space with *me*-me.

And I realized that older me was the other voice in my head. As for *me*-me, I felt myself getting fed weird moods by my other half. Not only was I too stunned to freak out, I was actually going along for the ride, like, being led around on a leash willingly. And I couldn't stop myself because—I guess I wanted it.

This is where you can hide for now.

I rolled my eyes and then surveyed my new location. "God,

isn't this typical?" I blurted out, shaking my head. "How much more classist can people be, expecting bad guys to come from the projects? Jeez!"

The place where I was directed was the swanky part of Vintage City. I stood—seriously filthy, torn up, and disheveled—in the middle of endless rows of sparkling clean terraced houses, with shiny, expensive cars parked in front. It was a familiar sight, yeah, with all the sanitized prettiness that made the neighborhoods what they were. The extreme contrast to where I'd first hidden myself hurt my brain.

Even more so the thought that Vintage City's superheroes, those expected to uphold justice and peace, would expect to find me lurking around in the poorer areas like that grungy old building and not think about froufrou places like this.

I guess Eugenics could do a lot to a person's genes, but it sure as hell couldn't do much for anything else, least of all a tendency toward snobbery.

You're a mess. Clean yourself up and then rest. You've had enough for one day. You'll have more time to explore your powers in days to come.

I'd never been big on crime. Then again, I'd never really committed one. A minor no-no here and there—a reluctant lie to my parents regarding my after-school activities the day Peter tore up my locker, snarky exchanges with my older sister, a joking request for Althea to break into the school's computer and change my Chemistry and Geometry grades. Oh, and that martini party with the Trill's gang inside their limo. Those were smaller than small potatoes in the criminal world.

At this point in time, given my new powers, I was ready to up the ante. I flitted over to a ritzy hotel nearby, spied on different rooms in the back of the building, and used my powers to weaken the window lock and break into one room that was unoccupied. Seriously, this energy wave thing was pretty handy to have. I was in there, totally enjoying a nice, warm shower, complete with the typical citrus-scented shampoo, conditioner, and soap. My soiled clothes bugged me when I stepped out of the tub. I washed them as best I could—and without laundry detergent—scrubbing as much of the dirt off my shirt and jeans as was humanly possible under the circumstances. Ugh. This definitely made me develop a better appreciation of our washer and dryer at home.

Speaking of, insta-dryer! I lined the dripping clothes along the tub's edge, all neat and spread out, and blasted them all with my energy waves. Voila! Dry laundry! I told myself to put together a running list of what I could use my powers for, in addition to drying clothes, opening squeaky doors, and encasing pesky superheroes in energy bubbles.

I stood before the mirror for some time, taking stock of myself physically. I expected a few changes in the way I looked now that I was, well, one of them—and wondered how obvious these changes would be to everyone who knew me. Especially my family.

Still tall, still pale, but—hey!—better built. Now how the hell did that happen? I'd been doing my pushups for some time, with really pathetic results. All of a sudden, I had muscles? All because my brain waves enjoyed a form of mental steroids? Well, I'll be damned.

I continued my survey. Hair still neatly trimmed, but the blue streaks had vanished. My face looked a little more angular—mature, maybe? I couldn't say for sure, but it definitely gave off a sense of age. Like my other half—the one that was kind of manipulating me right now—was showing himself physically. My eyes startled me. My irises had changed color from green to hazel, with a thin but distinct edging of red. I blinked several times, squinted, and leaned forward for a closer look till my face was practically pressed against the mirror.

Yeah, my eyes were different. What the hell? My skin crawled at the sight, but at the same time, I couldn't help but feel a major thrill. Gone was the old Eric Plath, I thought. Gone were the stupid grades, the stupid haikus, the stupid sensitivity toward perfection. The boy who stared back at me was better, way better. He was older, stronger, smarter, more independent, and he bowed to no one.

He had control over his life. Cliché would have me go further and say he had control over his destiny. A seriously dumb cliché, but it worked in this case, and I was shocked but in a more positive way. Was he also manipulating me into embracing this "new me"? Then again, I'd always wanted this, hadn't I?

Do you like what you see?

I slapped a hand against my mouth to keep myself from crying all of a sudden.

I pulled away, took a deep, relaxing breath to get a hold of myself, and walked over to the bed. I tumbled in, exhausted. What if the hotel manager let out this room to a new guest? I yawned against the big, soft pillow as I curled on my side, burrowing under the nice, clean sheets. Let them take it from me. I could crush them if I wanted to.

I didn't even know which part of me thought that.

CHAPTER 12

THE CRAPPIEST THING about being superhuman is just that—I was still human. I woke up after a couple of hours, my stomach gurgling and shrunken. I might be comfortable and totally hidden in my spur-of-the-moment hideaway—note to self: find a good place for my headquarters—but I was still broke and hungry. Crap. Crap, crap, crap.

So how did superhumans get around this sort of thing? The bed felt way too good, so I burrowed deeper under the covers, inhaling the scent of fresh laundry and ignoring my rapidly shrinking oxygen supply, while I mulled things over.

Peter still had to bow to his parents. Maybe Trent did as well. Althea got grounded, too, and was always arguing with Mrs. Horace about curfews and stuff. What about me? My family still had no clue about my transformation—no, *evolution*—that sounded better. It was most likely they'd still make me take out the garbage and help with the chores.

I didn't know how to go about things. My powers never came with instructions.

You do have a teacher.

"Yeah, but I have to break him out of that insane asylum just to have lessons," I grumbled.

Quit bitching. You owe him this.

I sighed and emerged from the cocoon of blankets, taking in deep gulps of air. "I need to go back home and eat," I said, staring at the ceiling, which was now being swallowed up by growing shadows. "I also need a change of clothes." Was I entitled to wear something fancy like Peter? Maybe the Trill would help me find something suitable. I honestly hadn't considered the idea of wearing Spandex. I shuddered at the thought of my gawky-ass body in stretchy, airtight material. Talk about being a huge disappointment to average gay boys everywhere. Of course, that little detail only served to ground home the fact I was one of the bad guys.

"I'm a supervillain?" I breathed, frowning. No. A protégé. Big difference. At any rate, was I supposed to be scared by that? Something deep and kind of distant stirred at the idea. Discomfort? Fear? Maybe. For the most part, though, I toyed with the idea and let it sink in, bit by bit, expecting violent resistance from my conscience but finding none. It was a bit of a surprise.

"I'm a supervillain protégé," I repeated and then whistled. "Wow."

Well, I figured being an up-and-coming supervillain was way better than being a dull no-name with nothing to boast about but a lifetime of average-ness. And a dull no-name who kept getting left behind by his superhero pals. The perpetual outsider looking in. Yeah, it was much, much better to be a supervillain protégé. At least I was finally on par with Peter and everyone else. Then discomfort stirred again, and I went back and focused on another, maybe the most important, reminder.

I was now two people in one body. Or one mind, divided and yet obviously conscious of each other. Things suddenly became clear. The day of the attack at the theatre, I had alternating halves surging to full awareness, one after the other: my tweaked side and my natural side. It was no wonder my natural self reacted with extreme and unexplainable fear to events I couldn't remember in full detail.

My tweaked side was in control during the theatre incident as well as the downtown attacks. Yeah—the one that felt older to me.

After waking from my nap, my natural side had emerged even more, kind of reasserting itself in my head. But my tweaked self was still there, not wanting to be suppressed like before, and I could see everything that happened now. From start to finish, I could remember every moment.

Now, lying in bed and coming to terms with my destructive capabilities, my two halves were at play. On one hand, I knew I was doomed to be on the wrong side of the law, and it freaked me out. On the other, I knew I was given a gift despite its dangerous source.

I was dangerous, too, but I was also special and much better than most people out there. I was terrified of what I'd become, and yet I reveled in my new powers and the possibilities they offered me, the doors they opened, the roads they revealed.

Another thought crossed my mind. With two opposing forces fully awake and sharing space in my mind and body, did it mean I was meant to be one of those torn, tragic figures in superhero myths? That I was both good and bad? The kind people were afraid of but admired at the same time? I couldn't tell. It was too early to say, and I didn't have the ability to see that far. The questions being left unanswered drove me crazy, but there was time enough for further thinky-thoughts. In the meantime, practical matters needed to be addressed.

Hopefully my parents wouldn't notice too much of a difference. I had to live with them for a while, after all, before striking out on my own, possibly squatting at the Trill's, considering our connection.

You're good at this!

"Maybe it comes with the powers."

And what about me and Peter? How would my newfound badness affect our relationship, which was pretty delicate to begin with? I couldn't think of an answer. In fact, I didn't want to and shoved the thought aside with a gloomy little huff after a moment of fumbling for something. Technically, Calais—no, Peter—and I were still together, but once on the battlefield, we were aligned to opposing forces. I'd be changed, my loyalties moving away from what had always been expected of me and my good, law-abiding, average kid-ness. Just from our near one-to-one that day, I saw that I'd be ruthless against him despite our day-to-day connection, and I was sure Peter would be just as relentless if he didn't have a choice. I hoped, in my own desperate, clueless way, this situation would make our bond stronger. God, did any of that make sense?

"As long as we don't have to fight each other, I guess."

That's a stupid thought. You know you'll have to fight him.

"I don't want to," I ground out. "Never. I didn't have control over myself back then, when I blasted him with an energy bubble, but I'm aware of everything now. I'd rather die than hurt Peter, and if I'm forced to face him, I'll let him beat me to a pulp."

A very stupid thought.

"I won't fight him. I'll never fight him. I still have control over this, and I can choose what I'll do in a battle. If you wanted me to be full-on evil, you should've taken over my head completely."

That was the key, wasn't it? If the Trill really wanted me to be his protégé, his mindfuck methods should've completely erased my old self, or at least squashed it into silence for the time being, and I'd be out there still, wreaking havoc up and down Vintage. As it was, I *did* have a choice in this still, even with my other half pulling the strings now and then. I could control this. I *had* to.

I continued to mull things over. By that time, a shaky confidence had taken hold of me, softening my fear with glimpses of hope. Maybe I could make my either-or situation work for me—that is, channel my powers and develop them for their purpose—which was destruction—but twist them as needed and use them for good. Technically I was a supervillain protégé, but I wasn't genetically-altered or hardwired into being a bad guy. Unlike Magnifiman and the Trill and everyone else, I enjoyed independence with my powers, and though they were meant for evil, I still had the freedom to turn the tables.

You idiot.

Hope surged in me. Yes, that made sense. I could live with the idea of being someone who straddled good and evil, even braving misconceptions about my true purpose. Being gay, I'd long grown used to slurs and misconceptions. I had the best of both worlds within my reach, and all I needed to do was to keep my mind fixed on my goals.

"I can make this work," I muttered. "Yeah, I can. I have to. I'll turn the tables on the Trill now I've got the chance." The voice in my head said nothing.

I forced myself out of bed and washed up again, taking care to make sure I looked as neat as possible, and hoping that Mom wouldn't notice the telltale stains and tears on my clothes.

I was never good at hand-washing clothes.

I exited the same way I entered, through the window. I flew past a row of ritzy rooftops before descending and walking to the nearest bus stop. I had enough loose change on me for bus fare; unfortunately, only one bus drove through upscale neighborhoods for its route, and it didn't go anywhere near my house at any given point. I had to get off in some middle-of-the-road area outside downtown Vintage and walk the rest of the way home.

Traffic was a nightmare, thanks to what had happened earlier. The main drag that cut through the shopping center was closed off. People in the bus chattered about the "big showdown" between Calais, the Fire Girl, and the Shadow Puppet's puppets. Half the passengers pressed their faces against the windows to catch glimpses of the closed-off street whenever the bus drove through one that paralleled it. I thought I saw a thin gray mist—smoke, most likely—hovering in space in the general area, and I guessed Fire Girl must have been busy even after I'd escaped the scene. Magnifiman never showed up when I was there. Maybe he was too busy fighting the Puppet elsewhere.

When I reached our front door, I stared at it, feeling nervous. Hopefully I'd be able to pull this off without a hitch. I fished around my pockets for my glasses, which I'd completely forgotten till that moment, and put them back on.

"Oh, damn," I hissed. It was awful. I pinched my eyes shut against the massive distortion and wondered how the hell I was going to make it through the rest of the day, practically blinded by the very thing that was designed to improve my eyesight.

I should come up with a good enough excuse to sashay around without my glasses. In the meantime, I needed to somehow find my way to my bedroom without causing myself any major damage. Sighing, I fumbled for the door and opened it after a moment of poking my house key all over the door just to find the stupid lock since I couldn't see it.

I stumbled inside. Literally. My foot got caught on the rug, which I didn't see, of course, and I nearly fell on my face.

"Eric? Is that you?" Mom called from the living room.

Oh, boy.

"Here we go," I muttered, straightening out my clothes and squinting against my glasses. "God, this is so screwed up." I threw a hand out and felt my way to the living room door, where I expected my parents to be, watching late afternoon TV. Liz was likely out with friends or upstairs in her room, yakking on her phone.

"Eric? Where've you been?"

I eventually reached the living room and looked inside. Everything was a mess of blurry shapes and melting colors. This was going to be harder than I thought, but I forced a smile.

"Hey. Good to see you guys. You two look great! Just fantastic!" I hoped I wasn't overplaying my hand.

"Why are you squinting?" Dad piped up from somewhere. He must be the dark blob at three o'clock. "Is there something wrong with your glasses again?"

"No," I said, laughing. "It's a little dusty out there, and something got in my eyes. I need to get to the bathroom to wash it off."

"You're a mess! What happened? Did you and Althea go downtown?" Mom demanded. "Eric, you two could've been badly hurt! What happened there is on the news right now!"

I raised my hands in a gesture of peace. I wasn't sure, but Mom was very likely the dark blob that squirmed a lot at four o'clock. "Mom, chill! I'm okay! We're both okay. Althea and I got separated when the attacks began—"

"What? You what? Got separated? How?"

Oh, my God, the blob grew. She was coming for me. I held my position, though. Superhumans never gave others an inch, and I was sure of that—note to self: ask the Trill about the Supervillain Handbook for good pointers and then sneak a peek into what I could do to turn the tables on him, the manipulating asswipe.

"Mom, come on! It got really crazy fast, so we followed the crowds and then got separated. I'm okay, see?" I made a show of looking down at my clothes, which were nothing more than this bizarre blur of denim, orange, and white—I'd worn my favorite rugby shirt, and it was now ruined. "A little dirty, but I'm in one piece. I don't even have a bruise."

I doffed my old jacket, pushed up my sleeves, and stuck out both arms, turning them left and right to prove my point.

"You're still squinting."

"Debris! And it hurts! I need to get it all washed off."

I tried to widen my eyes to look normal despite the awfulness of peering through my glasses. Oh, God, that hurt. I clenched my teeth.

"Okay, go ahead and get yourself cleaned up and ready for dinner," Mom replied, but something in her voice left me unsettled.

"Thanks, Mom. How's the garbage situation?"

"What about the garbage? Is there another strike? I didn't hear a word about that!" Mom blob directed her attention to Dad blob. "Honey, did you see something in today's paper about a strike?"

"No, no!" I cried. "I meant our garbage."

I thought I heard someone scratch his or her head. "You're asking about our garbage situation?" Mom echoed, sounding baffled. "You're actually interested in it?" All right, I must've overplayed my hand at that moment—note to self: work on finesse and remind Mom to cut back on her coffee intake.

"Uh, our garbage looks nice and healthy, Eric," Dad said. "Thanks for asking, though."

I nodded and grinned—it was actually more of a grimace, considering the agony I was going through, but I had to play my role to perfection—waving a hand at the two dark blobs in the living room. "Cool. Later."

With that, I felt my way toward the stairs and gingerly put one foot in front of the other as I ascended. I could've taken off my glasses then and simply trotted off to my room, but I figured my mom would likely have tiptoed out to the hallway to watch me. She was suspicious, for sure. The tone of her voice stayed with me, placing me on full alert.

Even with my left hand feeling the wall to guide me, I still managed to stumble a few times, nearly smashing my knee or shin against the steps once. Chrissakes, this sucked. It must've been two decades later when I finally reached my bedroom door. I suppose this would be one good reason against taking over the attic for my private sanctuary.

I crossed the threshold without trouble and immediately pulled my glasses off the moment I closed the door behind me. I sagged against it and pinched my eyes shut, allowing the dull pain to go away.

"Why couldn't I just have plain 20-20 vision?" I muttered. "This super-acute eyesight's going to be a pain in the ass if I have to pretend to be normal around my family."

It came with the package, unfortunately.

I shook my head and walked over to my closet, flinging my glasses onto my bed. "Now I have to figure out how to disguise that. This really blows, you know."

Everything was still in red and yellow, which meant I was in full tweaked mode now. Half of me withered at the thought that there was definitely no going back. The other half shrugged it off and instantly fell into a comfortable, relaxed state as I fished around for clean clothes. I really needed to get used to this. Actually, I really needed to take control of both halves and make them work together because that was the only way for me to see my plans through. When I stepped inside the shower stall for my second all-body cleaning, I was humming.

The way I easily adjusted to things, especially those involving danger, at least, continued to surprise me. Maybe that was one of the positives of being a supervillain protégé. Was that a show of total epic confidence? That would be cool. It meant I was stronger than before.

The old Eric Plath was definitely gone. Oh, and look—I could even sing an aria in the shower even though I never studied Italian. I never listened to opera, but I knew I was singing something from *Rigoletto*. Whatever the hell that meant. I dug around some more, pulling stuff out from some uncharted corner in my mind.

La Donna é mobile. Whatever the hell *that* meant.

I repeated the piece, my voice growing louder, sounding more and more different, and I knew it had nothing to do with the steam and the water. It was a man's voice, almost. All right, so it was nowhere near a tenor's range—Pavarotti? How'd I know that? I'd heard the name before but knew nothing about him. Still, things, strange and foreign, kept pouring out of me. God, this was weird.

Was there a significance in the song? Why did I sing it all of a sudden, given all the familiar rock songs I knew? Maybe it was worth the time and energy looking it up online. When I got out and dried up, wiping the mirror with my towel, I stared at myself—again in surprise.

Yep, I definitely looked different without my glasses, and it wasn't the absence of my glasses that affected my appearance. I'd seen myself countless times before sans plastic frames, and I never looked like this.

I really seemed to have aged somehow, and it was nuts. More muscle, more definition, a certain light in my eyes that made me think, "This dude knows a lot more than I do." I didn't know if I could get used to this. I was sixteen, not eighteen. I wasn't ready for this kind of change.

Take it easy. You're coming into your power, and it's showing physically. Just let it go, the same way you let go of everything else. It'll all work out in the end, all to your benefit.

I swallowed. "I guess." I must admit that I sort of felt like a stud. A pretty upset stud, but a stud all the same.

My eye color had changed back to its normal green, but there was still a distinct edge of red around my irises. I figured the change in color from green to hazel was affected by my being actively in "power mode." I was at rest now, so the transformation was gone. Yeah, I guess that made sense.

"Okay. Okay. Calm down, Plath," I whispered, closing my eyes and willing myself to relax. I reminded myself what I'd planned to do with all this. I hoped I knew what the hell I was doing, considering I was still kind of vulnerable to being led around by my other half. This was like being worse than wishy-washy. It was more like wishy-wishy-wash-wish-washy. Jesus.

I dressed up and rested, turning my attention to my window every once in a while. Peter was likely still busy out there. Althea wasn't in my computer. I wouldn't be surprised if she were still working with Peter and Trent. As for the fire girl, I now wondered what godawful name she'd be baptized with when the news came on later that evening.

I yawned and stretched, feeling so, so relaxed and satisfied. The issue concerning my glasses stayed unresolved, though. I pretty much spent the rest of my time working around that. I tried to neutralize the lens with my powers, but it did nothing.

"Oh, man," I sighed, staring at the damn things for the

longest time. "I guess that means my powers can't alter things on a molecular level or something like that."

Correct. It can damage inanimate objects but not destroy them completely. You've seen how it works. It's something like a cloaking mass of warm energy. It won't harm people or animals, but it can sweep them off like a wave or encase them in a bubble. You've used that, remember, when you cloaked the door to keep it from making a sound.

I nodded. "Yeah, I remember. That's pretty cool. I like my powers." I absently fingered my glasses. "But that doesn't help me at all in pretending that my eyesight hasn't improved."

Well, you're as blind as a bat.

"I know, I know. Shut up. That still doesn't change the fact I've gone from being virtually blind to having way better than normal vision. Seriously, why do things have to go from one extreme to another? I could've worked pretty well with a pair of glasses on my face."

Not really, no. Super-acute eyesight is a requirement in the superhuman makeup. Some people's vision will be much sharper than others, but compared to average folks out there, yours are abnormally keen. You can't do anything required by your powers with poor eyesight. It's too incongruent.

"Well, I'm going online," I huffed, throwing my glasses aside again. I was dying to find out what the media, local media, that is, was saying about that afternoon's adventures. Hell, I wanted to know what they were saying about me.

Computer turned on, twenty different windows opened simultaneously, and I was soon basking in newfound glory even though I kind of hated myself for it. I know, right? Like I said, wishy-wishy-wash-wish-washy. So fucking hopeless.

"New menace interrupts battle in downtown Vintage!" seemed to be the consensus.

I sat back and began to kick my brain into coming up with a proper name for myself. Bambi Bailey was notorious for baptizing the good guys, which meant I was free to design my own identity. At the moment, I was sure she was hard at work trying to figure out what to call Fire Girl.

After several minutes of nothing, I decided to distract myself temporarily by checking out the RPG community to see how far my alter ego had gone.

Sure enough, Energy Boy was straight, and he was also a bit of a pervert. He'd hooked up with three supervillain girls on the sly, all of whom looked like a gaggle of totally gothed-out Jane Austens in skimpy leather dresses. Apparently, Energy Boy also harbored an unrequited passion for Fire Girl, whom no one could touch because she was seriously too perfect for anybody.

CHAPTER 13

LESSON NUMBER 4,596 in Superhuman-ness: never say never. It took me some doing and a really shitty headache, but I managed to alter my glasses to nothing more than a neutral pair of faux eye gear. In other words, I ended up melting my glasses into a shapeless thing of plastic after I blasted it over and over again with little energy bursts.

In addition to being a crappy failure, the process was horrible. I couldn't say for sure how long it took me to mess things up, but it sure felt like a damn eternity—twice over, at that. I just concentrated while adjusting the energy waves that came out of my head as needed, despite earlier warnings there was nothing I could do with prescription plastic lenses.

Touch and go. Trial and error. For who the hell knew how long. By the time I was done with it, I nearly fainted from the strain and the pain it caused in my head. And my glasses were completely destroyed. Go me.

Don't say you weren't warned, you brat.

"Look, at least I tried, didn't I? That accounts for something," I shot back, my voice muffled against my pillow as I lay face down on my bed. Close to death, I'd like to add.

You forced your powers into a function they weren't meant to have. You could've done yourself worse damage. Something akin to a really bad hangover is the best you can expect from a stunt like this. Permanent brain damage isn't an exaggeration.

"But I didn't go that far. Now, shut up so I can rest."

Your powers reset themselves after a forced alteration like that. You won't be able to remember how to manipulate it to your preference next time. Considering how annoyingly stubborn you are, that's a blessing from this end.

"I don't care. I've got dummy glasses in my dresser somewhere, and I'll use them. That's all that matters now. Yay, me. Now shut the hell up, will you? Superhumans need some rest, too, after doing something like this."

If you're not careful…

"Yeah, yeah, I know. Nag, nag, nag. Now go. Shoo. You're bothering me."

Good grief, was I the only superhuman who was stuck with an independently-thinking voice-person-thing in my head? I sure hoped not, or I'd sue for a badly-handled power evolution process. If this voice-person-thing was supposed to act as my sidekick or the evil twin of my conscience, I was going to have a few choice words with the Trill about that. Note to self: see if a real sidekick could be recruited for me, because that would rock, bad guy or no bad guy.

The voice fell silent—thank God!—and I sought the comfort and healing powers of sleep despite knowing dinner was going to be served soon so I only had half an hour, tops.

I WAS BRILLIANT. Have I mentioned how brilliant I was? I was brilliant with a capital B. Liz woke me with a sharp kick to my bed—typical. I washed my face, combed my hair, and trotted downstairs in my dummy glasses. No squinting, no feeling around like a blind person, no stumbling, no bruises. It was fantastic.

Those glasses were part of an old Halloween costume I'd worn, but I totally dug the way the frames looked and ended up keeping them. They were pretty close to the shape of my now-destroyed glasses, so I was sure no one would notice the difference once I wore them.

I also dressed the part—strategic camouflage, yep. I made sure to change my clothes to an old, oversized shirt and loose, scruffy jeans to hide my sudden muscle development. Under those horrible, faded balloons, I looked about ten pounds underweight. I could do nothing about the angular lines that added age to my face, but I gambled on how they were pretty subtle.

Besides, I was sixteen and in the middle of an awkward growth period. That was a good enough excuse. My eyes were green again—as I was sure they'd shifted to hazel during my eyeglass-altering moment—and the red edging wouldn't pose a problem to anyone, what with the camouflage offered by my frames and all.

I loved myself. I'd never felt this pathologically narcissistic ever.

Even better was dinner itself, which wasn't different from any other meal my family enjoyed.

The only thing that was changed a little was the topic of conversation, which was firmly fixed on the incident in downtown Vintage that afternoon, and which I was heavily grilled over.

I answered everyone's questions with just the right amount of awe, horror, and shock that I could manage, and no one was the wiser.

"So, did you see the new villain?" Liz asked as she doused her salad with about a gallon of dressing. Ew.

"Kind of," I replied, not batting an eye while poking my fork around my plate for some candied pecans hidden under all those salad greens. I should've been given an Academy Award for my performance. "People were running everywhere, and there was kind of a crush where I was headed."

"What'd he look like?"

I shrugged. "Tall, I guess—I couldn't say for sure how

muscular because of the confusion, but he was floating by the founder's statue, and he glowed. Oh, and his eyes were white. It was really creepy." Peter's descriptions of me when I attacked the Elms Theatre came in pretty handy.

Liz listened to me with a deep frown. "Damn. Now I wish I'd gone downtown today."

"Then I'd have two of my children in danger, not just one," Mom retorted as she leveled my sister with a look that would've withered a redwood on steroids.

"So, uh, what're they saying about this new villain?" I asked, making sure to widen my eyes in a show of squeaky-clean innocence. Parents, especially mothers, loved that. My mom was especially vulnerable, and when she turned to me, she practically melted in her chair. I was still her baby, oh, yes, I was. I could milk this for all I was worth.

"Not much right now," she replied after giving me that look that went *Awwwww*. "Just the same things you mentioned, Eric. Want some brussel sprouts? I know you can't stand them, but they're steamed, and they're good for you."

Yikes. Did superhumans talk about mealtime ordeals like this during club meetings or something? I kept my cool, though, seeing as how Mom's earlier doubts when I'd first arrived home had vanished completely. If she noticed something totally bizarre before, she didn't see it now. Go me. As long as I didn't overdo it, I'd be able to keep my charm meter at full throttle, and no one in my family would know what hit them.

"Can I finish my meat and potatoes first, please? There's no room on my plate, with my salad and all." Eyes wide and sparkling, enhanced subtly with a long-lashed blink or two. I was five years old all over again, and if I kept that up one minute longer, I'd give myself diabetes.

Unfortunately, Mom looked to be on the verge of a massive cute attack, so I backed down a bit.

"I mean, I can only handle so much rabbit food."

Mom's eyes narrowed. Bingo.

"So it looks like the Dark Side is catching up with the heroes, number-wise," Liz piped up. "Let's see. The Devil's Trill, the Shadow Puppet, and this new energy kid. They're all up against Magnifiman, Calais, Spirit Wire, and that firestarter girl. Bad guys need one more to their number for an even match." She paused and grinned broadly, sweeping the table with her gaze. "This is exciting! I don't know how many others are coming out of the woodwork, but I expect that in the end, it'll be a balanced match between the two sides. Awesome."

Dad cleared his throat and sneaked a peek at the clock. "Fifteen minutes till the news," he said. "We'll find out what's up. I'm sure by the end of it, we'll have names for the new girl and the new boy."

I coughed violently and had to take a few large swigs of my water. That was what I forgot to do! Shit! A manifesto—or else, like the Puppet, a calling card or two. Damn! Damn, damn, damn! Bambi Bailey was going to latch on to my identity, slap my butt with the King of Crap Names before I could establish myself properly.

"You okay, Eric?"

"Yeah, I'm—I'm fine, Dad." Cough. "Thanks." Cough.

It was my turn to wash the dishes that night, but I asked for a bit of a delay, so I could watch the news with my family. Mom, still reeling from my earlier assault on her motherly senses, would've granted me anything. After dinner, she gave me a fond, dazed grin and a quick peck on the cheek for an answer. Then followed that with a playful mussing up of my hair. That was definitely a yes.

In the living room everyone huddled—except for me, anyway, as I stood by the door to ensure a quick getaway in the event of severe shock or distress over Bambi Bailey's baptism. While suffering through the commercials, I comforted myself with one nefarious supervillain plan after another, stuff that I could do tomorrow after school—note to self: replace stupid, pointless haikus in writing journal with outlines of Bad Guy Deeds; I was still an intern and needed to learn how to be more hardcore.

Then I could use them against the Trill when the moment came.

Ah, yes, there she was. Dressed up, hair held together by ten cans of hairspray, but rather than looking heartbroken, Miss Bailey was once again glowing, starry-eyed, at the camera. I also realized her beauty mark had vanished. Maybe she'd run out of those faux moles, finally.

Behind her sprawled the carnage from the early afternoon. Snarled traffic, abandoned cars, smoke rising in pillars all over the place, people wandering out of shops to gawk at the scene that graced a three-block stretch of Main Avenue. With the sun still up, I imagined the report was taped immediately after the incident. Cops swarmed the area as well, and flashing red lights from a gazillion squad cars that had crammed the area after the attack gave the scene a bit of a surreal disco quality.

"Looks like this is a rerun of today's Breaking News report," Dad noted with a loud yawn and a cat-like stretching of his arms above his head.

"Huh. So much for breaking news," Liz snorted.

"It all started when Vintage City's Paragon of Virtue received an alert regarding a possible break-in at the Department of Antiquaries', well, Antiquaries Department. Along with Calais and Spirit Wire, Magnifiman foiled the break-in attempt, but it appeared as though the whole thing was a two-tiered job." With a triumphant toss of her head, Miss Bailey turned to her side, and the camera panned out to reveal—yep—Magnifiman standing next to our intrepid reporter.

Appropriately angry, beautifully glowering at both his seductress and the camera, Magnifiman stood in all his brawny, justice-keeping glory. Massive, monolithic chest thrust out as he took on the pose of Vintage City's gallant protector with his arms akimbo, his cape fluttering slightly in the breeze, his hair just this side of mussed—he was a vision. I wouldn't be surprised at all if he were to be the cause of a sudden wave of boys realizing they were gay on this day alone.

"Thank you for staying with us for a moment, sir," Miss Bailey cooed. She flashed Magnifiman a pale, womanly throat as she threw her head back in order to look him in the eye.

"Well, I'm afraid I can't stay too long, Miss Bailey. There are leads to follow in addition to petty crimes to thwart," he replied. Never had I heard impatience sound so sexy in that low, silky purr. It was hypnotic. It was seductive. It was...

"Damn it, Peter, where are you?" I hissed, squirming a little in my too-baggy jeans.

Easing the pressure of surging hormones made me resort to nail-biting. Seriously, even Magnifiman's cheesy dialogue style couldn't douse the fires.

"Of course, I understand. If you don't mind filling us in with some of the details..."

Gross, did she just swipe her tongue over her lips?

Magnifiman, as usual, didn't seem to notice. He merely sighed and nodded before turning to the camera, his eyes, already narrowed to near slits, shrinking even more. Superhuman vision aside, I highly doubted if he could see through those muscular slivers.

"The Shadow Puppet has left us a number of calling cards—most of which are harmless, nothing more than the usual expression of pathological narcissism that's common among criminal minds—"

I nearly choked on my nails and had to muffle my sudden fit of coughing behind my hands.

"—there are, however, a number of these calling cards that are actually coded messages."

"Coded messages?"

Magnifiman nodded again, his slit-gaze unwavering. It was a little infectious, to be honest. I caught myself a few times narrowing my eyes in response to his look. "Yes, coded. I can't tell you what the original calling cards say since all that's classified information, but this I can share—and I'm talking to *you*, Shadow Puppet, as well as the good citizens of this good city!" Magnifiman gave the camera an emphatic jab of his oh-so-muscular finger. The fury of a man of virtue was plain beautiful to watch on camera—more so in person, yessiree. A hundred and one gay boys up and down Vintage City must've just swooned from an overload of a hundred and one different fantasies about this glowering, threatening hunk of superflesh at that moment.

"The noose is tightening, you vile fiend!"

Oh, the high romance of his language! A breeze blew again, the hair and the cape all fluttering in a show of angry, virtuous defiance! Shakespeare, eat thy heart out!

"Calais and I got to the place in time to find several of his nefarious dolls hard at work in breaking the security code. Spirit Wire was able to delay them, but a short-circuit broke the connection between Spirit and the Department of Antiquaries' computer."

"Oh, my!"

He nodded—for the third time—his jaw clenching. My gaze automatically dropped to his chin and its magnificent cleft. Then it moved farther south to his Adam's apple. For one crazy moment both halves of me thought how much being on the wrong side of justice sucked.

Stand your ground, soldier!

I snapped out of it and started chewing on another finger.

"Yes, Miss Bailey. Spirit Wire's delay helped, and I was able to come after several of them while the rest broke ranks and retreated. As it turned out, they'd responded to a signal that made them turn their destructive designs on the innocent folks of Vintage City. Calais went after them, and so did our new ally, whom we were honored to fight with, side-by-side, this afternoon." He paused to look long and hard at the camera. "Young lady, though you've heard this from us before, I want to say this publicly. You're an asset, and Calais and I thank you."

"As do the rest of Vintage City," Bambi Bailey piped up. "Thank you, Miss Pyro, for your courage!"

Miss Pyro. That was definitely impromptu. Miss Pyro was lucky it didn't take a lot of thought, or she'd be baptized with something like Fiery Whiplash Femme or something.

Magnifiman stared at Miss Bailey for a moment, suddenly at a loss for words. "Yes, very well," he muttered. He turned his attention back to the camera just as Bambi Bailey gave him the biggest, brightest, toothiest smile this side of heterosexual courtships. "This is not to say, however, that the job's done. The noose might be tightening, but Vintage City is still under many threats from the most despicable criminal minds to be born."

"Created in a lab, you mean," I muttered against my tattered fingernail.

"You, young man, will be found out," he growled at the camera, his muscular finger once again teasing me. "Yes, *you*, energy fiend! Someday soon, you'll slip up and leave an energy trace, and by all that's good and right, we'll have you where we want you! You will—and I swear this—feel the hard hand of justice tightening around you!"

My breath caught, my cheeks heating up. "Really? You promise?" I gasped.

I had to lean against the doorway, my gnawed finger limply caught between my teeth as I stared at my nemesis and brother-in-law in a lust-filled daze. Magnifiman was threatening me on camera. I never felt so—so wanted—and in public, too. All this time I thought I'd gotten over my crush on him. Then again, I did notice I'd been rather hormonal lately. It was like PMS for boys, but way, way funner.

"Any idea who this new threat is, Magnifiman?"

I finally remembered how to breathe.

"No, but we'll find out, Miss Bailey. I promise you that. He attacked Calais and the gi—Miss Pyro with his energy waves. Even the police weren't safe from him. He tried to help the Puppet's mechanical henchmen, but we don't believe he works for or with the Puppet."

"So, did the Puppet get away then?"

Magnifiman smiled grimly. "He was never there. Two of his walking dolls are in captivity right now. They'll help us with the final pieces of the puzzle."

Bambi Bailey gave her hair a quick pat as she turned to face the camera. "The people caught in their cars during the attacks today are doing well, we're told. In shock, of course, but they're all fine. It seems the bullets that were fired at them were these strange bullets that vanish on impact."

"Excuse me, Miss Bailey. I must attend to the needs of Vintage City."

"Of course. Thank you, Magnifiman," she said. Magnifiman didn't even bother to wait. He simply took off while she was still talking, but all the same, Bambi Bailey appeared to take it all in stride. I figured she was happy enough to have him with her for a while, considering how long she'd been waiting for this moment. She merely looked back at the camera and continued.

"Yes, where was I? Oh, strange bullets. No one yet knows what these bullets are made of, or what kind of damage they can do to the human body. As of now, what we do know is this: the bullets are capable of breaking glass and denting metal surfaces, but they leave nothing behind once they come in contact with objects. Strange though this might sound, but they really do seem to vanish on impact. People were lucky to be shielded by their cars this afternoon. Police and investigators have scoured the crime scene, but they failed in finding anything that they can examine—almost as if these bullets never existed, except for the fact they left clear physical damage where they struck…"

That was enough torture for one evening. At least I wasn't named—this, I discovered before I went to bed, when I sneaked downstairs for an illicit late night snack and caught Liz doing exactly the same thing; it was a brother-sister gossip moment that I was afraid would ruin my reputation as an up-and-coming, tormented supervillain. I left my spot at the door and washed the dishes, the drudgery of what I had to do easing my fluctuating hormone levels. It sure brought me back to the depths of average-ness, but I figured that was a necessary evil if I wanted to be incognito.

"Superhumans deserve more dignity than this," I ground out as I dumped the garbage afterward. To add insult to injury, I nearly got savaged by a moth that had decided to claim our garbage can lid for its moonbathing perch. Superhumans needed to start a union. I seriously had to organize one.

CHAPTER 14

I WISHED MY dad had saved that newspaper with the Trill's manifesto. I was hoping to put one together of my own, but I'd no clue what went into it other than "Hello, I'm So-and-So, you all suck, I'm going to destroy this city, and Magnifiman's a wuss!"

Of course, I could always break the Trill out of the asylum, but I wanted to do this on my own. I expected him to have plenty of chances once he was out to mold me into the best supervillain I could be—before I used everything I learned against him, yeah!—but in the meantime, there were a few things I'd rather do, myself. What better way to test my abilities than to exert some independence?

So I stayed up late that evening, half-killing myself over my manifesto. It was like writing another essay for my English class, and I was going nowhere fast. Why didn't supervillain manifestos come with Literary Cheat Sheets?

Althea never possessed my computer. I figured she was caught up in all the excitement that day unless she was avoiding me because she somehow found out I was energy boy. Peter also didn't show up for a romantic visit. It was easier for me to come up with reasons for his absence, but that didn't bother me as much. I had enough things to do as it was.

You're trying too hard.

I grimaced. "Do you come with an on-off switch or something? I need to focus here, not listen to some nagging voice in my head."

It seems that you don't fully understand my purpose for being here.

I waved a hand and glowered at the computer screen. "You're here to piss me off, and you're doing a pretty good job of it. I'll give you a raise when I can afford to. Now go the hell away. I'm busy."

The voice stopped, and for a moment, I was surprised at how quickly it responded this time. Maybe it was one of those signs of my taking more and more control of my powers. God, I hoped so. This whole wishy-washy-badoozy thing was really wearing me down. I shrugged things off and moved forward. The blank file stared at me, defiant and mocking in all its snow-white, virgin state. The cursor seemed like a tongue that kept sticking out at me—the way some snot-nosed kid with missing front teeth would do to random people. Neener-neener, yep.

Minutes ticked by, and still nothing. This was writer's block at its worst, and I wanted to destroy something. Of all the times for it to happen! I stood up with a curse and paced around my room, grumbling and hissing as I stared at my bare feet and my bedroom's faded old wood floors.

I couldn't even figure out a name for myself. How stupid.

I must've worn a circular path on my bedroom floor before I forcefully reminded myself what was at stake here. In other words, I stood before a wall and knocked my head against it a couple of times. Then I tiptoed downstairs—dazed and head-ache-y—for nutritional reinforcements. Within moments I'd sneaked back in with a cup of Dad's coffee, which was nowhere near decaf, and oh, boy, did that work!

Funny how stress, pride, and a deep, crippling fear of Bam-bi Bailey's naming skills worked together to push me into a state of caffeine-induced stream-of-consciousness brainstorming.

Energy waves. Warmth. Asphyxiating bubbles. Organic bruising, no death or maiming. Limited inanimate destruction. Sci-fi stuff. Television. Reruns, retro crap whose scripts I'd memorized by my fourteenth birthday. Cheesy, cheap special effects. Aliens and monsters. Bad acting. Star Trek. Vulcans were cool. Romulans were cooler.

"That's it!" I crowed, my spirits perking up as I rushed back to my computer and typed out my new supervillain alias.

The Cloak.

I grinned, feeling giddy and official and ignoring the throbbing lump on my head. Romulans used cloaking technology. My powers could be used for cloaking. That was simple, to the point, and appropriately ominous. I squirmed in my chair, unable to believe my luck, not to mention my cleverness. Of course, I'd yet to crash through the wall of writer's block, but I figured the surge of jubilant energy would carry me through the godawful process of coming up with a good manifesto.

I cracked my knuckles and set to work, channeling what I could of my initial euphoria. The words came out slowly at first—awkwardly and painfully—but I felt untouchable then, and I kept going, wholly unfazed, and before long I was lost in a fury of superhuman angst. I stopped when I felt I was done and sat back to reread my rough draft. It worked, I thought, not a bad first effort from a newbie bad-ish guy.

I almost—*almost*—threw in a couple of threatening haikus, but that would've given my identity away—note to self: stop sharing your poetry with Peter and the rest of the Quill Club.

Besides, haikus would be too artistic for someone as hardcore as The Cloak. I took a quick break and went downstairs again for another cup of coffee. Sure, it was eleven o'clock or somewhere around that time by then, and I was sure setting myself up for a night of miserable sleep deprivation, but I could afford to sacrifice peace and rest for one night. Business first, yep, pleasure and everything else came a distant second.

By the time I was done, it was three in the morning. I was dizzy and alert in a residual sort of way, the kind of alertness that wouldn't go away because one's nerves had been hopelessly fried by too much caffeine at the worst time of the day.

Screw all that, I thought, eyeing my manifesto over and over. I set to do something and got it done in excellent time. It had been revised a few times since, and I was satisfied with it now. I saved it and resolved to drop it on Bambi Bailey's lap the next day. No use waiting for the papers to be printed and distributed. Live, breaking news was more immediate and more effective.

Besides, I knew where the local TV news station was located, and I could always corner Miss Bailey at the right time.

I tumbled into bed, turning off my light, and curled up, wide awake still, but oh, well. I felt quite impressed with my ability to wade through the psychotic quicksand of superhuman-ness with some ease. It was going to be a tough balancing act being an ambivalent superhuman type, and I reminded myself not to be overtaken by the Dark Side despite my desire to learn more from it.

Like I'd noticed a few times before, gone was the old, stupid, average Eric Plath, after all. Part of him was still there, though, with my good half probably acting as a check to the impulses of my tweaked half. Double the pleasure, double the fun—in a good-bad sort of way. That was all that mattered, and I told myself that again and again as I stared into the darkness.

Keep my head on straight. Never give completely in to the Dark Side.

ALTHEA LOOKED LIKE hell in the morning. I caught her leaning against her locker, her forehead resting against it, her eyes closed. I expected to hear her snoring, but her eyes fluttered open on my approach.

"Hey," I said.

"Hey." She yawned.

It was kind of weird, but despite my mental and physical fatigue, I was in pretty high spirits that morning. "I lost you yesterday," I noted, leaning against another locker as I watched her struggle with hers. Not that she was trying very hard, anyway, seeing as how her eyes had slid shut, and she was just feeling around the dial for her combination. "Looks like you got away without a problem."

"Yeah. I had to run to the nearest ATM to access a computer, but I overshot myself and pretty much broke the bank's system. You saw me."

I made a face. "Yeah, so did the rest of the world. You were exposing your identity. Bad move."

"I know, I know, my bad. I got carried away and didn't think. Anyway, I ran back home, which is kinda sad. It sucks that I can't just surf the wires without being attached to some dumb computer. You know, just stand anywhere, focus my powers, and then BAM! I'm wired. I'm hoping I'd reach that point sometime soon, when I advance some more with my powers."

"Hey, from what I saw on the news last night, you were able to delay the break-in." I slugged her playfully on the arm. Althea teetered on her feet, but her eyes were still closed, and she was again leaning her forehead against her locker.

"Yeah, I guess. Not good enough, though. I wanted to manipulate the Antiquaries' main security codes and trap all the dolls in one place, make it easier for Peter and Magnifiman to smash them to bits." She yawned, pulling herself away and knuckling sleep from her eyes. "So, what about you? Where'd you go?"

I shrugged. "Got swept up by the crowd. It was a mess. I'm still surprised that I saw the whole thing even with the stampede and craziness that went on."

"Oh. You saw the new guy then?"

Althea blinked several times and fixed me with a clear-eyed gaze, her head slightly tilted to the side. I tried, for a fraction of a second, to read her and to see if she knew something.

Unfortunately, a fraction of a second wasn't enough—note to self: work on comprehension speed.

"I did, yeah. The news reports pretty much summed up the scene—or what he looked like." I gave another shrug, pretending indifference. "Have you talked to Peter?"

The first bell rang, and Althea turned her attention back to her locker. She managed to keep her head clear for a little while and finally got her books out, and we walked to class together.

"Hell, I haven't been talking to anyone else *but* Peter!" She chuckled. "After the attack, he contacted me from the police station and had me analyze all kinds of data he and Magnifiman uncovered."

"All classified, I'm sure."

"Duh?"

I rolled my eyes. "So you guys were at it all day then?"

"Pretty much, but we had breaks. Oh, the new girl was with him, too."

"Miss Pyro?"

Althea stifled her laughter. "Her, yeah. God, I wonder how she took to her new alias. Anyway, she stayed with Peter the whole time. Pretty cool, huh? It's almost like a superhero league that's forming. All we need now are people with wind, electricity, water, and sound powers. Peter and I were too busy talking shop, though, so I wasn't able to say much to her except 'Hi' and 'Later.'"

I barely listened to her as I gnawed at my lower lip. "So, uh, do you know if Peter's around today? He never called me last night, but I figured he was pretty busy." Of course, I didn't expect him to spend the entire day with Miss Pyro.

"He's around, yeah. I saw him earlier today. He was in a hurry, and he was busy talking to someone on his cell phone."

"Probably Magnifiman—or his mom."

"Probably." Althea paused and gave me a quick, searching look. "Hey, have you been working out lately?"

"Yep. Can you tell? Push-ups and some weight training every day, though I wish I had the right equipment for them."

Althea grinned. "I'm impressed! You're doing pretty good for someone who doesn't have the right stuff."

"Yeah, well—improvisation's one of my talents." I sure wasn't lying to her then.

Peter was in his seat when we entered the classroom. The air crackled with excited chatter among the students, with "Miss Pyro" and "Shadow Puppet" being the morning's buzz words. As I neared my seat, I saw that Peter was still on his cell, his back turned to me, one hand pressed against his other ear. I didn't bother him and just took my spot, reluctantly forcing my attention to mundane crap like school. My manifesto was safely tucked inside one of my bag's inner pockets, and I was itching to pull the disc out, ogle it, and brag to anyone who'd listen that, ayup, I'd just taken one step closer to full-fledged supervillainship. Of course, that also meant having the entire class and two incognito superheroes jump me when I wouldn't be ready for them.

Peter eventually got off his phone, but only because the second bell rang. He put it away in his backpack and turned to me with a tired little smile. "Hi," he said. "I'm sorry I didn't call you yesterday."

I waved him off despite a faint—but not *that* faint—wave of annoyance that swept over me when he spoke. "That's cool. I expected you and Trent to be up to your ears with work."

"Yeah. It was nuts."

"So when did you get home?"

"I don't know. Sometime around ten, I think."

I stared at him. "No way. You guys were working all that time?"

He smiled sheepishly. "Pretty much. We took a couple of breaks to eat, of course. Trent went off for a power lunch type of thing with the mayor and Sgt. Bone, and I took Wade out. Then we went to dinner later on."

"Wade? Who's he?"

"She." Peter glanced around and then leaned a little closer, his voice dropping to a whisper. "Miss Pyro. Her real name's

Wendy, but she hates it and prefers to be called Wade."

I looked at him for a moment. "Oh, okay," I eventually blurted out. "Hope you guys had a good, productive meal."

"We did, actually. I was sick of talking shop after so many hours holed up after the attack, knocking our heads together to get some puzzles solved. So dinner was fun—probably the most fun I've had in a long time."

I nodded. "Cool."

"By the way…"

I raised a hand. "You won't be able to see me or talk to me for a while because you're busy."

"Yeah. Sorry." Peter laughed quietly. "Now that Wade's working with us, the group's moving forward pretty quickly in nabbing the Puppet." He paused as I turned away to fumble around in my bag for my books and notes. "Wade's pretty cool, Eric. You should meet her sometime."

"I'm sure she's a charmer."

"She's really sweet and cute—though a little insecure still, but I'm helping her get over that. And she's really, really smart. Probably one of the smartest people I know. Once you start talking to her, you can't stop."

I nodded at his backpack. "I take it you were talking to her just now?"

"Oh, yeah," Peter snickered, blushing. "I didn't realize how much time had passed. I wasn't even aware of walking to the room. I was totally lost in conversation with her."

"Sounds like fun."

His eyes sparkled, and he spoke in a light, hyperactive whisper. "She's like me, Eric."

"Uh—gay?"

He laughed, knuckling me playfully. I hated getting knuckled, and he knew it. "She's just as torn about having powers as I am, you goof. It was amazing talking to someone who could actually empathize with me. Once we started complaining, everything just came out, and neither of us wanted to stop."

"Sounds like you guys puked all over each other or something."

"In a way, I guess. It was like all these pent-up feelings and shit about what we are and how we fit in and what we're supposed to do, yadda, yadda—suddenly the dam burst. It was like free therapy for both of us."

I cocked a brow at him. "Peter, you know you could tell me anything. I never kept you from confiding in me."

"I know, I know, but this is different, though. Sure, I can tell you things, but I still can't really, you know, tell you everything. Our experiences—who we are, what we are—" he faltered and fumbled with his words, flushing deeply as he struggled. I nodded, sighing.

Yeah, I wasn't capable of empathy and all that shit because I wasn't a fucking superhero.

"I know what you mean. It's okay. You don't have to say it." I forced out a reassuring little smile, which seemed to work. Peter's confusion and embarrassment gave way to an expression of relief. "I'm glad that she was able to hear you out."

"I can't tell you how relieved I felt afterward. I was tired but also energized, in a weird sort of way. I almost asked her out to a movie."

I rubbed my temple. "Oh, I'll bet you're dying to kick that new guy's butt for attacking her yesterday." I glanced at him and smirked at the cloud that darkened his face. "Yeah, I was there yesterday and saw the whole thing. Didn't Althea tell you we were hanging out when the attacks happened?"

"She did, yeah." He looked angry, his jaw setting. "Everything happened so fast when he got Wade, the coward. I didn't recognize him at all. He was just glowing all over, too, so it was like being blinded by light right before he hit me with his energy wave. Bastard. I can't wait to find him."

I stared at my notes, my pen held in one cold hand. The world was once again in red and yellow. "Better watch what you wish for," I murmured, my words drowned out by that day's lessons.

CHAPTER 15

SCHOOL WAS WORSE than a drag that day, and I was convulsing in joy when it was finally over.

I hung out with Peter and Althea at lunch, and it was one of the biggest mistakes of my life. The conversation was mostly shop talk, from which I was completely excluded—naturally! The buzz centered on the formation of a superhero league when more good guys came into their powers.

So what were the requirements of this hypothetical elite club? Superpowers, of course, all used for the good. Intelligence, the smarter, the better, seeing as how the current known good guys were all rocket scientists in their own ways. Wade went to a private school outside Vintage, where she was an honor student. How she'd managed to keep Peter on the phone for such a long time while in school was a mystery to me, but I guess such was the nature of privilege.

I could barely take a bite of my homemade sandwich with all the synaptic energy that crackled around me through lunch.

There were a number of things about being on the wrong side of justice that I wasn't so sure about since I'd undergone my transformation. Sorry—evolution. All the people I cared the most for were on the side of good, and while I enjoyed masquerading around and pretending to be my old, stupid, insignificant self, I now found myself faced with more pressing concerns about my allegiances, my private schemes of turning the Dark Side on its head, and my concession to a possible lifetime of ambivalent superhuman-ness.

That day, I desperately wished my good half didn't exist, that it had been wiped out once the tweaked half had stepped out. The problem was that I continued to feel pain, and it sucked. I shouldn't feel hurt at being pushed aside by my own friends. I shouldn't feel regret at having to choose between my family and the Trill, even if it were only to move my scheme forward. Even if the feelings that overcame me since Peter talked to me that morning vacillated quite a bit, I was surprised I still had to experience pain just by listening to his fanboy jabber over Miss Pyro.

If I was supposed to be with the bad guys, shouldn't I be numb to all these? Wasn't that how supervillains became so good at what they did—because they simply didn't care? Maybe that was an indication that I ought to break the Trill out ASAP, so he could fix me some more, and I could carry on without an unwanted emotional jolt every once in a while. My good half was a little too good, I guess, and it was hell not being able to suppress it when I needed it.

I let Althea and Peter enjoy their conversation and slipped off into silence for the entire lunch period while they chatted right through me. It wouldn't have mattered, I guess. If they included me in their superhero talk, they'd be patronizing me in the worst way. If I got pissed enough and outed myself to them as the New Bad Kid on the Block, they'd literally kick my ass—unless I got to them first, of course, but I was in the early stages of my evolution and was still a little iffy about my powers and their use.

Sometime in the course of my Lunch of Torture, my gaze

strayed to my hand and the friendship bracelet Peter had given me. It was still there—still intact, unscratched. Not a piece of computerized—or radioactive or whatever—fiber out of place.

"Hey, Peter, is this thing still working?" I asked, breaking up their privileged circle of two. I raised my arm and flashed him the bracelet.

"Uh, yeah, it should be," he replied. He looked momentarily confused. "Though I'll have to admit, I haven't been checking up on you lately."

"Too busy, I know." I shrugged and pulled my hand away. "That's cool. I was just wondering."

"What's up? Are you thinking of ripping it off or something, so you can join the other side?" He laughed.

I looked at him and then at Althea, who was laughing along. I smiled my fakest and shrugged, turning my attention back to my sandwich. "Sure. Why not? Life's more interesting that way, don't you think?"

That earned me another round of patronizing laughter. Maybe they didn't think I was smart enough to be a bad guy, even. I'd expected as much. One of the biggest fears I'd had since finding out about Peter and Althea was my falling short of their standards, and look what was happening. I'd gotten used to holding back, though, and whatever ache I felt the whole time was eventually ignored. If anything, I was beginning to learn to accept it. I'd read somewhere there were people sometime in the past who swallowed small doses of poison day after day in order to make their bodies or systems immune to the stuff or to pain. I never bothered to check the accuracy of those claims, but thought they sounded morbidly romantic. I figured if the Trill failed to harden me against hurt, it would be best to absorb what came my way in order to reach that point in my development.

That's very clever of you.

I smiled grimly against my sandwich. Maybe my powers made me smarter.

"ALTHEA, WE'RE GOING to need your help tonight," Peter said after school when we were hanging out at Peter's locker.

"After homework, of course."

Peter laughed. "Well, duh! Wade and I will call you."

"Oh, she's coming over to your place?"

"Yeah, to meet my family and have dinner with us. Dad and Trent will be around. Mom and Dad can't wait to meet her."

"I'm surprised her parents let her go."

"Well, Mom called them and asked them herself, apparently. Just this morning, too, when she was at work. Wade just left a message about it." Peter raised his cell phone as though to prove it. "She thought she wouldn't be able to, but I guess Mom put on the charm for her sake." He chuckled.

I stared at him. I'd never seen him in such a bubbly mood that lasted all day. "That was quick. How long did it take for me to be invited to dinner with only half of the family?"

Peter rolled his eyes. "Jesus, Eric, don't be petty."

I sneered. "I was just kidding. I'm glad they're taking to her very well."

"I am, too."

"The way you're talking, Peter, I wouldn't be surprised if you end the day being engaged to her." Althea snorted. "I hope she knows you're gay and really, totally taken."

Peter was about to say something, but stopped and glanced at his watch. "Oh, shit. I gotta go. Wade's showing up early, so she can help me work on my speed and agility."

Tennis lessons, it looked like—those agility training moments that I used to be involved in.

Funny how love worked.

"And I promised to help her work on her aim. She's still pretty rough around the edges. But, yeah, we'll call you, Althea."

Hopefully Wade wouldn't burn the house down before the dinner bell was rung. I followed them to the parking lot, my pace slowing while theirs seemed to speed up, matching the hyper conversation that continued between them. Watching them from behind, I felt clarity bloom. The non-existent distance between them—in intelligence, abilities, connections—couldn't be any more clearly demonstrated than in that one slice in time, when they walked side-by-side, totally wrapped up in their shared experiences and their shared language so that the rest of the world just didn't exist. I pictured Wade forming a third figure, walking to one side of Peter, sandwiching him between two girls who were his equals in everything.

Eat it up.

I did. I welcomed it, absorbed it, let myself go in the bitter aftertaste. I stopped, and they kept going farther and farther, completely oblivious to the fact I wasn't with them anymore.

Eat it up. Use it.

I turned around, hurrying away and taking a different route out. I never looked back, but I swore to myself if I suffered a momentary weakness and shed a tear over this, I'd allow myself that since it would be the last time. Where I was headed and where I belonged, there was no room for useless crap like grief, was there?

Good boy.

I PACED OUTSIDE the Yoshiko Kagawa building, where Channel 3 News was housed. Common sense, or the lack thereof when I formulated my scheme, once again stared me in the face. I had my manifesto in hand, and I didn't know exactly how to get it to Bambi Bailey without exposing myself in the most obvious way possible. If I had the money, I'd have it sent by special one-day courier or something, but I was some dumb high school kid with no job. Well, a job that paid, anyway.

You really should get the Trill out and have him help you with these technicalities.

"Look, how can I expect to grow if I have to keep leaning on someone for what I need? Besides, this identity thing has nothing to do with him. This is all about me."

Well, you're obviously not going anywhere right now.

"Shut up. I'm thinking."

Wake me up when you figure something out.

Yeah, like I had any choice to begin with. I shook my head and gave my skull a slight thump with my hand. After a few minutes of pacing, I decided to withdraw before I got picked up for loitering or for being a terrorist. Besides, the security guy was beginning to give me that I'm-Watching-You-Bucko sidelong glare. Just as I was walking away, someone left the building and headed in the direction of the row of coffee and pastry shops across the street. I recognized him as one of the cameramen who ran around after Miss Bailey. He looked like he hadn't slept in weeks, and I could only guess he was on his way for some super-caffeinated beverage and a bag of super-sugared junk to keep his hours as sleep-deprived as possible. He'd brought a book with him—a fairly large hardcover volume, which would work for me.

I followed him, my disc ready for planting. I'd made sure to use a permanent marker when I labeled it with Miss Bailey's name and "urgent" appended to it. A sticky note wouldn't have done the job, the way things were unfolding.

He entered the jam-packed Mediterranean Café, which was perfect. I'd easily melt into the crowd. My heart beating wildly, I shadowed him till he was inching his way through the crowd, his head turning left and right as he searched for an empty table. There was none. He got in line—a fairly long and slow-moving one, at that—and I immediately shifted to Plan B.

I stood behind him, completely ignored by everyone. The café swarmed with late afternoon caffeine addicts. There was constant movement around me, which would camouflage what I needed to do.

I quickly opened the CD case and popped the disc out,

inching closer to the guy as he took to reading his book while waiting his turn. His jacket pocket was within easy reach. With my heart pounding at a near-murderous rate, I reached out and carefully slipped the disc inside his pocket, staying long enough to make sure it disappeared inside the half-yawning slit.

He stepped forward when the line moved, and I stepped aside, nearly getting tangled with a couple of girls who were trying to get the hell out.

"Hey, watch it!" one of them cried.

"Sorry, sorry."

I pushed past the crowd, glancing once over my shoulder to make sure I wasn't being followed. Nope, I was safe. The guy stayed pretty oblivious, and the two business suits who stood behind me were too busy yakking away, sharing a newspaper between them. I didn't breathe a massive sigh of relief till I was two blocks down the road.

I was getting really good at this. I nearly laughed. Hopefully the cameraman wasn't so spaced out that he'd smash my disc before he'd even reach Bambi Bailey's office. If he screwed up my plan, I'd cloak him real good.

"Okay, so cloaking might not sound threatening enough, but I'm capable of being hardcore," I muttered, slowing my pace to an idle one as I made my way home.

The rush hour crowd swelled, and I was suddenly weaving my way through the bleary-eyed, swarming mass. So many of them were too tired to be more aware of where they were going, and they kept bumping against me, muttering "Oh, sorry" as they pulled away, only to walk straight into someone else. That I didn't sport bruises when I arrived home came as a surprise.

It wouldn't have mattered, anyway. I was too fixed on my manifesto and whether or not Miss Bailey received it. With everyone still at work or in school, I ran up to my bedroom and threw myself into homework, glancing at the clock every ten minutes to make sure I was making good progress. I desperately needed to be done with everything by the time dinner was being prepared. If I was slowed down by something, it was an occasional distraction caused by thoughts of Peter.

Stay strong!

"Yes, sir," I muttered, gritting my teeth as I forced my mind on Chemistry.

I didn't bother to see if I finished my homework in record time, but it sure felt like it. Mom and Liz had arrived home by the time I was done, and Mom was hollering for me to get my butt downstairs and help out in the kitchen.

I washed up and dressed down. I'd just stooped to pick up my clothes from the floor when I noticed something sticking out of my jacket pocket. I dropped everything and pulled it out.

It was a note, scribbled on expensive-looking stationery. I blinked stupidly for a second or two before unfolding it.

I need to speak with you. Go to the antiques shop tomorrow after school. Oh, and don't even think of using your powers on me. Brenda Whitaker.

That was my first coronary that day—Peter's fanboying of Wade didn't count. How the hell did she know about me? And how did she get that note inside—oh. Swarms of people, many of whom were bumping into me. She must have been one of them, and I wasn't even aware of it.

Pretty clever of her.

I mulled over the note for a bit longer, my initial shock melting into determination. I wondered if she had powers as well. I suppose I could set my powers on standby or something to that effect, ready to go just in case. Of course, I'd absolutely no clue how to do it, but I could always spend the rest of the night practicing.

I sighed heavily. "I'll figure something out in school, I guess," I grumbled, crumpling the note and tossing it away. The strain of last night's caffeine frenzy had long showed itself, but it seemed that I'd only then grown aware of it. By the time I made it down to the kitchen to help Mom with dinner, I could barely keep my eyes open.

No matter. The anticipation of that evening's news was enough to carry me through the tedium of dinner and the horrible exhaustion and dizziness that came with lack of proper sleep. Liz stayed behind to do the dishes, so I got to watch the news without having to bargain for time.

When Bambi Bailey appeared before the camera, I held my breath.

"There's been a very important development involving Vintage City's new threat," she said, looking elegantly grim under all that makeup and hairspray. "This afternoon, a disc was delivered to my desk…"

My heart skipped as she recounted the arrival of my manifesto via her cameraman. I started chewing a nail, my skin prickling as I listened to my own words being read off to the camera. The thrill of being introduced to the city on live TV was incredible. A quick glance in my parents' direction kicked up my excitement even more. They both stared at the screen in super rapt attention, eating up every word I wrote. True, my manifesto was one-third the length of the Trill's, but I'd learned to be concise after all those haikus I'd written.

Within moments Miss Bailey had reached the end. This was it. My triumph over her. My assertion of independence via a simple process as coming up with an alias. It was going to be a beautiful, beautiful moment.

"…and the manifesto, ladies and gentlemen, was signed. Our new threat has a name."

I grinned against my chewed-up finger. Go on, lady. Say it.

Bambi Bailey hesitated, drawing the tension out a little longer. God, she was good. I wondered if she took acting classes or something.

"It's signed, the Clock."

Time froze. So did I. Even Mom and Dad turned to look at each other, totally confused. The *what?*

Miss Bailey looked up at the camera, a slight crease forming between her brows. "I don't understand why he'd be called the Clock, but that's how his name's spelled." She shrugged weakly. "It's allegorical, I think."

CHAPTER 16

"A GAME—THAT'S the world to them. That's all they think about. Games."

"So you think he's just screwing around with us?"

Peter shot Althea a frown. "What else can we expect from sadistic bastards like them?"

"Oh, I don't know," Althea replied with a shrug, pausing only to take a sip of her orange juice. "Sometimes I wonder if we're giving them more credit than they deserve."

"Supervillains aren't that stupid. I mean, we've second-guessed ourselves a dozen times over the Trill and the Puppet, and it drives me nuts. Just when we think we're on to something, they throw us a curve ball. And I hate being proven wrong when it comes to serious stuff like this."

Althea snickered, rolling her eyes. "How can naming yourself 'the Clock' be a diversion? That's a pretty dumb way of throwing your enemies off."

"Yeah, it could be nothing more than a simple case of a typo," I snapped as I glared at my lunch, which stayed untouched. It *was* a typo. God, I wanted to beat myself to a pulp so badly.

"That's even stupider than I thought." Althea laughed. "A typo!"

"I don't see anything stupid about that. Dumb shit like this happens every day. Do you see red squiggly lines under 'clock' when you type it? Hell, no! It's not a misspelling, so how can the stupid program catch it?" I shot back.

Althea waved a hand to shut me up. "Oh, jeez, Eric, chill out. It's not like those idiots would care what we say about them. All they want is to screw up our lives and come out on top, period. They're programmed to be psychopaths, remember?"

"I still think it's too simple a reason," Peter cut in, wiping his mouth with his napkin.

I glared at him. "And what does Wade think?"

"I haven't talked to her yet."

"Since when?"

"Since this morning, before I left for school."

"Hoo boy, that's a record."

It was Peter's turn to roll his eyes at me. "God, will you grow up? I'm not sleeping with her, if that's what you're trying to get at."

"Thank you. It's always good to get that out in the open," I returned. What control, I thought—my voice staying calm and level, my heartbeat keeping to a pretty steady rhythm. I did notice my arms, which were tightly crossed on my chest the whole time, felt stiff, my hands cold against my shirt. It was taking me all I had to hold myself back. all that pent-up tension from a horrible mix of shitty feelings since yesterday was collecting and growing in me, to the point that I could almost feel myself literally swelling up. My vision was also dangerously shifting to red and yellow, and it was getting harder and harder to control it.

Althea leaned over the table and formed a "T" with both hands. "Time out, time out, boyfriends," she said just as Peter opened his mouth to say something. "Quit getting your panties in knots. We're all in this together, remember, Eric?"

I held Peter's gaze all that time, hoping he'd read the challenge in my look. Somehow, something deep in me simply didn't care anymore. "*You're* in it together," I said. "I'm not one of you. Remember, Althea?"

Peter shook his head and broke the stare-down. He took a sip of his drink and directed his attention to Althea, and there it stayed for the rest of our lunch period. So they continued the conversation about the Clock and the possibilities behind his being a supreme genius or a sublime moron. I sat by while they debated over me, coming up all kinds of theories about my background, my personality, my IQ, my purpose for being a "sadistic bastard."

The Grand Canyon-sized space between us yawned several miles wider in the course of our, no, their, lunchtime conversation. It was one thing to come to some kind of realization regarding my place in their superhero lives while watching them walk out of the school parking lot, lost in conversation and completely oblivious to the fact they'd left me behind. It was another thing to be with them, up close, listening to them yak on and on about me: calling me names, making fun of my spelling skills, my sanity.

What irony.

There I was, pretty much their equal in superhuman capabilities, yet all the while still their inferior in everything else—morality, intelligence, personality, whatever. I'd bet the world the source of my powers was considered inferior to theirs, too. Mine was artificial, while theirs was genetically-enhanced. They were allowed to make mistakes while they worked on mastering their powers, and I was laughed at over a typo. Damned if you do, damned if you don't. That barely even scratched the surface of my real plans regarding my powers and how I planned to use them, but I figured at that point, what noble plans I might hatch—and all for their benefit, I might add—didn't really matter.

As far as they were concerned, I was nothing.

I managed to force a couple of bites of my sandwich down my gullet, if only to ensure I survived the rest of the day without going berserk over food deprivation and battered pride. I hated feeling all these. I deserved better. Tonight I'd have to sneak out and pay a quick visit to the asylum to see how I'd be able to break the Trill out. Then he'd help kill all emotions in me because feeling all this hurt and anger just plain sucked. I know I said it before, but it deserved to be said again. Besides, my tweaked half was growing tired of being incognito. The romance of independence living as a supervillain called to me, and I couldn't say no. Was that vulnerability hardwired into me, or did it have everything to do with rebellious adolescent hangups? I couldn't tell.

What else did you expect?

"I don't know," I admitted in a soft whisper as I walked to my locker. Peter kept at Althea's side. I could hear them still chatting away even from a distance and with the lunchtime crowd swelling around me. "I really don't. All I know is I'm going to go crazy if I continue like this, getting torn into two. I don't know where I belong anymore. The Trill screwed up big time. Why didn't he just go all the way and turn me into something easy and black-and-white like him? With these Eugenics babies, they're either good or evil. I'm caught in gray areas, I can't find my way out, and I hate every damn minute of it." I switched my books and went straight to my next class alone.

Listen, who wanted to exert his independence for a while, hmm? Who refused to listen to advice about getting the Trill out, so he can be properly trained? Hmm?

"I didn't ask for your opinion, smartass."

I took my usual spot in my English class, slumping in my chair and waiting for the agonizingly slow ticking of minutes. I didn't bother to look up when Peter and Althea walked through the door. I gladly ignored them the whole time.

Things stayed pretty chilly between me and Peter through the rest of the day. I tried not to think about his family and their eagerness and readiness to welcome Wade—a nice, smart girl who went to a private school. Mrs. Barlow herself called Wade's parents the morning after the Puppet's attack and invited her over. I couldn't even remember how long I'd waited for a date to be set, but at that time, it didn't really matter to me. Wade had already met Mr. Barlow and Trent, while I'd contented myself with a rain check because they were both too busy to meet me. Peter had found a kind of soulmate in her, given the strong parallels in their situations as superheroes.

No, I could never understand his issues because I wasn't like him. He could never expect me to empathize the way Wade could. All I could offer him was an open ear and a shoulder to cry on, not a real, deep, psychic connection that only someone with parallel issues could give.

And you know, what the fuck ever.

I suppose it was better to realize all this now than later, when I'd invested all of myself into a relationship that wouldn't have worked out in the end, anyway. We were too different. Even now, with my artificially-generated powers, I still fell far short, and I was just sick and tired of being the laughing stock of the elite few. It was either one way or another for me—no gray areas. None. Gray areas only left me wishing that I lived in another city altogether, where I knew no one, the slate was wiped clean, and I was still this stupid, dorky kid with glasses who couldn't save his Geometry grades if his life depended on it. I wouldn't care about obscurity in that case.

At least I'd be left alone, and I could be myself, and I'd be happy chilling with my family. Maybe I'd fall in love with a boy who was just like me, and he'd love me back without reservations.

I stared glumly at my notes.

God, I wanted to destroy something.

The hours came and went in a sluggish, reeking mass of whatever. After my last class, I hustled over to my locker, blindly did what I normally did when I stood in front of it, and hurried out. I didn't know if Peter or Althea tried to catch me, and I didn't care. If they were to catch me, it would be because I was helping destroy the city, and I needed to be thrown in jail.

Bitterness was a pretty addictive thorny pill to swallow.

Considering how broke I was—the story of my life, really—I just rode my bike to Ms. Whitaker's antiques shop, feeling silly at the thought that as a supervillain protégé, I was pretty pathetic on the incognito level.

"God, there I go, feeling miserable again. This has gotta stop," I ground out as I wove my way through traffic. Well, maneuvering my bike in a way that would make those crazy big city bike messengers proud was probably the only skill I could wear like a badge of honor. Anyone who'd seen me bunny-hop my way through the more pockmarked streets would agree.

I eventually reached the shop, after a nice, leisurely roll through semi-muddy streets, thick, sickly-hued steam creeping out of grates, and the familiar smell of decaying brick that couldn't hold on to its make-believe glamour. It was gross. The frightening thing was that it was also so comfortable and familiar. Bleah.

I hopped off my bike and walked it for the last block. I didn't even realize till then I'd no idea what to expect from the meeting; I didn't seem to care much either. I answered Ms. Whitaker's note as though I were off on some routine errand for my mom. I wasn't in a panic, but I guess I was still pretty bummed from the crap that'd been going on between me and Peter. If Ms. Whitaker had any hard liquor she could serve me in one of her antique goblets, that would be great. Even better if the goblet looked like the Holy Grail.

Ms. Whitaker stood in front of her shop, having a smoke, or at least she appeared to be. Dressed in another turtleneck sweater, tight jeans, and boots, she stood on the sidewalk with one arm crossed over her stomach, the other resting against it with its wrist relaxed and limp, cigarette lightly held between the fingers in a very intellectually blasé kind of pose. Thin tendril thingies of smoke rose, but Ms. Whitaker wasn't contemplating her surroundings at all. She stood motionless like that for some time, her head bent, her eyes fixed on the pavement directly in front of her.

There was a pretty healthy pile of shit on the sidewalk, directly in front of her shop's door. Someone must have been walking his or her dog, and it had a bit of an oopsie, which was never cleaned up. I swear, some people shouldn't have pets or children. If the price of antiques didn't drive Ms. Whitaker to close her business, shit on the sidewalk marking her shop's entrance probably would.

I approached her, and she glanced up. She didn't appear startled or peeved, just blandly curious.

"Someone should clean that," I noted.

She gave a faint shrug, took another drag of her cigarette, and turned her attention back to contemplating shit. "It's the city's job to do this, I think."

"Maybe we should call them—watch our tax money at work."

Silence fell on us for a bit. I wondered what passersby thought when they walked around us because we were blocking pedestrian traffic over dog droppings. Ms. Whitaker finally shook her head.

"Wow," she breathed. "This is *so* David Lynch."

"I'm sorry, who?"

She looked at me again, smiled wryly, and jerked her head in the direction of her shop. "Come on in, sweetie. You can bring your bike inside if you want. Just make sure it doesn't knock anything down, okay?"

I nodded and maneuvered my bike toward the door, which she'd propped open with a brick—probably pulled out of someone's wall. From light, I plunged myself into gloom and the creepy smell of age and lives long gone. I eventually found a spot for my bike—next to a narrow desk with a matching hutch, which I ogled for a while, imagining how the whole set-up would look in my bare old attic space. I tried not to look at the price tag, of course.

Ms. Whitaker called me over to the counter. "Do you like tea? I don't drink coffee, so I can't admit to being hip like you kids nowadays. I've got a bunch of different teas, though, and a plate of ginger cookies."

"Yeah, I like tea. Thanks."

She grinned at me as I shuffled over to the counter, eyeing her offerings more out of hunger—that day's miserable lunch had finally caught up with me—than suspicion. She could have drugged me, for all I cared. She'd set an old bar stool in front of the counter. I perched myself on it, staring at her offerings and suddenly feeling embarrassed by the whole thing.

On looking back, I now know it was a weird feeling to have when one had just been lured to a surprise meeting. I should've been on the alert, defensive or angry, even, ready to play all kinds of mind games if I had to. But no. I was kind of embarrassed, maybe even a little shy, and I squirmed a lot. My gaze flitted from one thing to another, unable to rest on anything for more than a second.

Ms. Whitaker sure noticed.

"I was right," she said after a moment's uncomfortable silence. She met my eyes with a curious, deeply probing look, but I didn't sense any malice or danger in her. "You're not like them."

"I don't understand," I stammered. No, I wasn't doing too well at all.

She raised a hand and lightly grazed my face with her fingers, as though tracing something only she could see. Wherever her fingers went, her eyes followed, all fixed and intent. It was all I could do to hold still and not sneeze when she tickled my nose—unintentionally. My thoughts momentarily flew back to those nice moments when Peter would trace my face with a finger before moving close for a long, deep kiss.

"Oh, damn it," I whispered, my hands balling into tight fists on my lap as I willed my fledgling boner to go down.

Ms. Whitaker pulled her hand away with a light chuckle. "Sorry," she said, turning to pour hot water out for me. "It was pretty forward of me to do that, I know. Don't worry, I wasn't trying to do anything illegal. I just needed to make sure of things, even though I knew I got them right the first time around. Want anything in your tea?"

"No thanks," I replied, tearing open a bag of chamomile tea. "I don't understand why I'm here." Now was the time to be on supervillain mode, I guess. I made a show of narrowing my eyes at her in a threatening way, which she appeared to ignore.

"You've changed a little since I last saw you," she said, drawing a chair up and sitting herself down. She plunked a couple of sugar cubes in her tea and stirred.

"What do you mean?"

"You look somewhat harder around the edges, a little older." Her eyes rested on me as she sipped her drink, the steam from her cup looking like a thin veil of white. "I'm guessing you now look the way you'll look about—oh—three years down the road." She paused. "Also a bit sadder."

I bit into a cookie—note to self: ask Ms. Whitaker for the store where she got those ginger cookies. "Isn't there like a disease that makes people age way, way faster than they should?"

"It's not a disease." She laughed, rolling her eyes. "Quit the innocent act, honey. You have powers, and you didn't get them naturally. You're an—"

"My name's Eric, not Olympia," I growled before blowing gently on my tea. "Last time I checked, Olympia's a girl's name."

"Olympia's just a name I give to artificially-enhanced types. Like you."

Okeedokee. Play along.

Hoping I looked totally confused, I blinked and munched thoughtfully. "I still don't get it. By the way, are these cookies on sale? I want to tell my mom about them."

"Honey, I'd know, believe me. I was a little older than you when my dad experimented on me the same way you were worked on. In your case, though, it looks like the method's been perfected." She smiled. "More tea?"

CHAPTER 17

I STARED AT her, drop-jawed. "Shut up!"

"Shut up about what? I was around seventeen when Dad messed with my head. Through suggestions, you know. Lots of them, embedded in tutorials he gave me on foreign language arts." Ms. Whitaker poured me more hot water. I was simply stunned at how cool and indifferent she was when she talked about her past. "I was home-schooled, by the way. Pretty convenient setup; Dad didn't trust the school system. I think it's safe to say he hated it. Ironic, really, seeing as how he married a teacher."

"Didn't trust the school system? As opposed to what?" I blurted out. "Screwing up your own kid's head with your so-called lessons?"

She set her cup down and leaned forward to fix me with a steady gaze. The shadows in her shop did nothing to soften the spooky lightness of her pupils. "Listen," she countered, "what Dad did to me was nothing compared to what's been done to you. His experiments had everything to do with knowledge absorption, not a distortion of someone's mind and behavior. If I understood the mechanics behind it, I'd be able to explain it all to you right now, but I don't. I was never aware of it until I started experiencing all kinds of weird things."

"Like what?" I was growing more aware that the gloomy silence around us felt grave-like. I caught myself glancing over my shoulder twice, shuddering. All around, the antiques stood half-covered in shadows like graveyard relics.

She took a dainty bite of a cookie. "I could see through people."

"You could see dead people?"

"Don't be funny."

"Sorry, sorry. I'm just feeling a little creeped out by all this." I waved a hand in the direction of the shadow-cloaked antiques behind me. "Your antiques aren't helping me any, either."

Ms. Whitaker sighed and rubbed her temples. "Some kind of…ability that I was born with was somehow enhanced. Developed. Matured. Know what I'm saying?"

"And that ability you were born with was, like, ESP or something?"

"I guess so. ESP, sixth sense. Sounds pretty gothic, doesn't it?" she said with a wry smile.

I frowned at my tea. "Sounds crazy, not gothic."

"I don't think it's any less crazy than your ability to destroy objects with energy waves created by your mind."

"Are you saying that I was born with these bizarre energy waves or something?"

"No. They're unnatural. They're obviously a manipulation of your mind. Maybe it's an ability that's been planted." She paused and considered, frowning. "No, scratch that. It's not a 'maybe.' It's definite."

I glanced at her sharply, and she just stared at me without blinking. "Eric, I tried to forget about everything and brush it all off as some freak accident that was unique to my experiences. After moving to Vintage City, though, and seeing what's been going on here, I'm now convinced it isn't true. Meeting you, especially, and reading about what recently happened downtown forced me to rethink my own conclusions."

"Can you start over, please? I'm having a hard time wrapping my brain around all this."

Chamomile tea wasn't helping me cope with its promised relaxing effects. I decided to up the ante and tear into two new bags of the stuff and to let them steep for twice the length of time as my first couple of cups.

Ms. Whitaker grinned and nodded. "Okay. I'm sorry for hitting you with this from out of the blue." She excused herself for a moment and vanished to her shop's back room, returning with a new box of ginger cookies. "These things are on sale at Bettina's Market. Your mom shouldn't have problems finding it. Eat up. You need the calories."

"Okay. Thanks."

She settled herself on her chair and tore the box open, dumping the cookies in a pile on the plate. I didn't need another invitation to dig in and swiped a cookie, sighing inwardly at the sharpness of the real bits of ginger that were blended in. Memories of Christmas from way back when coursed through my mind. Memories of happier, simpler times.

"Mom was a teacher, and Dad was a psychiatrist. They—"

"Wait," I broke in. "You mean…I thought your dad was a geneticist."

She stared at me for a moment, and my brain froze. Oops. I said too much, didn't I? "You know about the labs then?" she prodded, her words slow and cautious.

"Yeah, I do." I swallowed. Oh, great, did I just compromise my friends? "Only rumors, though." That was a quick and awkward save, and I could tell from the way Ms. Whitaker looked at me—looked right through me—that she didn't buy it.

She broke the clumsy moment by glancing past my shoulder and in the direction of the front door, which I was sure she could easily keep an eye on from where she sat despite the expensive junk that crammed the shop. Then she turned her attention back to me.

"I know about the labs, too, but no one told me about them. No one needed to, thanks to Dad. It's something I'm sure he didn't even consider when he experimented on me, that I'd be able to read his mind and know what he was doing, and for whom he was testing things out." She flashed me a humorless little smile as I stared at her, wide-eyed. "Strange how things work, no? Dad knew people from the labs, was friends with a couple of geneticists. From what I'd seen, he was consulted over manipulations involving human subjects. I'm talking about genetic manipulations, but I'm no scientist, so I can't really understand the nuances of the process and, God, anything scientific, I can't grasp!"

I nodded, sipping my tea. "I'm like that with Chemistry."

"Anyway, from what I could piece together, Dad began to look into mental manipulation because—again, I'm pretty much grasping at straws here—he thought the geneticists were onto something in altering the human makeup to enhance certain features and abilities. I don't know if he continued to work with them on the side, but I suspect he did as an advisor of some kind, and he did his own experiments to test things out."

"I can't believe he'd use his own kid for that!" I ground out. "Hell, I can't believe that he'd even consider screwing around with someone just to see if he can improve on her! He's no better than those crazy geneticists!"

She watched me, listened to me, with a little smile. Weirdly enough, I felt much more comfortable talking to her about this, compared to my discussion with Mrs. Barlow. I could only guess it was because Ms. Whitaker and I were on par when it came to our "powers," compared to Peter and Trent. She was no less superficially manufactured than I was. The difference was that she was the "prototype," and I was the "new model." Our experiences, though, stayed the same.

Just as Wade's experiences were the same as Peter's. I stared at the half-eaten cookie in my hand, my spirits sinking at the thought. Another parallel, this time in terms of inferiority of source.

...ad wasn't any different from most parents out ...ed me to be the best in what I could do. Unlike ...rents out there, though, he stumbled across a chance to cheat Nature, and he took it. He knew I loved history and foreign languages, and he used it."

"What about your mom?"

"She didn't know anything. She taught me at home, sure, but she didn't realize the extra study materials my father gave me on the side were heavily coded to work on my mind on a subconscious level." She sighed and glanced down, running a finger along her teacup's rim as she lost herself in thought. "I really don't know if it mattered had she known. Mom died in a plane crash when I was eighteen. She was on her way to visit an uncle."

"I'm sorry."

"Well, the long and short of it, Eric, is that Dad tried to make me 'better.' And I knew—I saw in his mind, little glimpses of his thoughts, that is—that he only wanted me to succeed in what I loved the most. You know, turn out into a summa cum laude in history or language arts someday. Maybe write several scholarly journals for Ivy League universities and so on. Win a Nobel Prize in something I was passionate about. His heart was in the right place, but his methods…I forgave him a long time ago. I guess I'm glad his experiments didn't really succeed beyond a certain point. He couldn't work his way past their limitations, it seemed."

I mulled things over, pulling out past conversations and weaving them into the present one, picking up a few threads and dropping others as I went. "That's how it all starts, isn't it?" I asked, my voice dropping. "Good intentions. Someone wishing a better future for his or her loved one. I guess in your case you're lucky it didn't go too far."

"I'm grateful for that, yeah."

"Did he stop? I mean, when did he think that he'd done enough?"

"When I began to read his mind," she said with a sly grin and a mischievous sparkle in her eyes. "At the same time, I didn't show much improvement in my absorption of facts. It was like he turned something on that he didn't expect while shooting way off the mark when it came to his actual purpose. Pretty bizarre."

I frowned. "Sounds kind of like Pandora's Box," I offered, and she burst out laughing, easing the seriousness of the moment. I couldn't help but chuckle.

"Yeah, you're right. It was, wasn't it? At any rate, when I began to finish his sentences for him and pull out odd bits of information that only he knew, he realized he'd gone too far, or at least done something completely unintentional. He stopped but never confessed to it. Then again, it wasn't as though he needed to, anyway. I already knew too much even if what I managed to get out of him were fragments that I had to piece together, myself." She paused and shrugged. "Things weren't the same between us from then on. I think I frightened him enough for him to keep his distance, and I was fine with that. When I turned eighteen and had enough money saved, I moved out the first chance I had."

She leveled me with another steady, intense gaze. "Know what's even more ironic? I majored in business when I went to college. And all this?" She waved a hand. "All this is what's left of my passion for history."

I'd already filled myself up with ginger cookies and tea, and I regarded her morosely. "I'm really sorry."

"Sorry? Don't be! I'd rather be doing this than be some mentally manipulated big name scholar who technically cheated her way to fame even though she didn't know it."

"So, uh, do you still have your—you know—powers?"

She nodded. "A little bit. Most of them are gone, but I retained some ability to read people. That's how I found out about you."

"How's your dad?"

"Gone. He died a couple of years ago, actually, but we were estranged till the last moment. I only heard about his death through a cousin." Ms. Whitaker raised a hand while sighing deeply. "I think that's all I'd like to share about my personal life. I'm a lot more concerned about you, Eric."

I shrugged, my earlier depression returning. "My situation's more complicated," I stammered. "You said earlier the process was perfected in my case. I guess I won't argue against that, but what can I do?"

"How did it happen?"

"Um—music. I was knocked out, and music was played while I was unconscious. I guess like you, it was coded or something like that, and it worked better than your dad's method, apparently. I mean…" I looked back at her, feeling hopeless. "I'm hurting people and destroying things, and I'm torn. I want to be better than I am, and in a way I got what I wished for, but look at what's happening."

Ms. Whitaker leaned forward and took one of my hands in hers. "Listen, I'm not saying that I know everything because I don't. What I do know, I figured out on my own, and even then, I'm still not sure about the veracity of my—my conclusions. Eric, you probably know way more than I do about those genetics labs, but what I understand, what I can see, is that your case isn't hopeless. You're not manipulated the way Magnifiman, Calais, and the others are manipulated. You're like me—Olympia."

I stared at her, beyond confused. "But I thought your name's Brenda."

"It is, and I want you to call me that, all right?" She laughed, her grip on my hands tightening as though in reassurance. I sure as hell didn't feel comforted. "I'll explain what I mean by that in a moment. The fact of the matter is your situation right now is superficial, just as mine was. Sure, your transformation's more complete, but judging from your behavior right now, I can see you still have the ability to turn things your way, not someone else."

I tried to look away, but she caught my chin with one hand and gently turned me to face her. "You're conflicted over all kinds of moral and ethical issues surrounding your powers, am I right? Okay, you don't have to answer that since I can see it, anyway. Do you know what that means? Your confusion? It means your transformation isn't as deep as it probably should be, at least compared to the ones who were manipulated on a genetic level. Whoever screwed with your mind could only do so much, and it shows. Because it's superficial, it isn't perfect even if it's more complete than my own experience. Do you hear me?"

I nodded, my vision blurring as the waterworks began. God, I hated crying. Especially when it happened in front of someone I barely even knew. "Yeah, I do."

"You don't have to go through with the transformation. You still have enough of your conscience intact to know what's right and what's wrong, and you can use it against your other self and—and, well, turn things around. Overcome the surface changes and get rid of them once and for all."

"You make it sound so easy," I said, fumbling for a napkin and blowing my nose into it. Loss of control sucks.

"Let me ask you this. Have you tried using your powers for something they're not meant for?"

I shook my head, turning away to rub the tears out before they embarrassed me any further. "No. I don't think I can…" I stopped myself when I remembered my melted pair of glasses. I also nearly told her my real plans of developing my powers as they were meant to be developed and then turning them against my "creator." I figured, while I trusted her enough, I was still better off not saying a single word about my purpose. I was in this alone, and I was going to see this through to the end, alone. The risks were high, especially those involving my immediate safety, but I was convinced I'd nothing to lose. Nothing left to lose, anyway.

She frowned and spoke with a slight hesitation. "I don't doubt that you can do it. You're not helpless against this, Eric.

You're not. Whatever happens to you in the end, it happens by choice. You know how I can be so sure of that? You haven't blown me away with your powers because I know too much. You could've. The chance was right in front of you, and it would've been so easy to kill me, destroy my shop, and walk away, pretending we've never met. You didn't, though."

"You told me in your note not to."

She chuckled. "Yeah, sure, but a hardened criminal wouldn't have cared. He'd still walk through my door, force me into a corner, make me talk about what I know, and then obliterate me."

"Okay. I'll keep that in mind." I'd managed to regain control by then and enough dignity for me to meet her gaze even though I knew I looked like some pathetic crybaby. "Thanks for talking to me. I never thought there'd be someone else out there like me."

She smiled, nothing condescending or patronizing or mocking, just a quiet, comforting little smile that could only be shared between two people who kept a secret. She reached out and tousled my hair. "I'm guessing that your powers take advantage of your insecurities. They feed off them. If you cling to them, you'll only pull yourself farther and farther away from your good side. Know what I'm saying?"

I thought of Peter again. "I can't help it sometimes. Being in his company's enough for me to think crap of myself."

"Whose company?"

I glanced up, an answer poised, but I could see she already knew the truth—or at least a pale shadow of it—so I just shut my mouth and had another cookie. Ms. Whitaker—Brenda—didn't press. She refilled my cup and continued to talk.

"You can't turn your 'mentor' in," she said in that straightforward, matter-of-fact way of hers. "Just as I couldn't turn in my dad back then. There's no way. We don't have proof, do we?"

"No, we don't," I said in a stronger voice. "I know I can't prove anything. I tried to tell people, but they found nothing when I was x-rayed and stuff. I've got nothing."

"Then you're on your own, Eric, but you know I'm here if you need help. There's only so much I can do, but I'll try." She paused and reached under the counter, pulling out a battered little book. "Here. Read this."

I stared at the faded and torn leather cover. "What is it?"

"You wanted me to explain the whole 'Olympia' bit. The answer's in here. You don't have to read the whole book. Just the first story. You'll understand yourself, me, even the others who've been manipulated differently from us."

I gingerly flipped through the yellowed pages and saw that the book was a collection of short stories from one author. I reached the first page of the first story. It was called "The Sandman" by E.T.A. Hoffmann.

CHAPTER 18

I READ THE story in one sitting and was blown away. Olympia was a walking doll—an automaton—more realistic in appearance compared to the Shadow Puppet's mannequin minions.

On a surface level, she made me think of the Puppet, but as I read well into the story, I understood what Brenda meant when she called me Olympia. I was one. Just as she was almost made into one. It was like, I was the Trill's son just as Olympia was Coppola's daughter.

What was a hell of a lot more disturbing was that I also found myself in the story's main character, Nathanael, and I wondered if I was also spiraling into craziness and destruction the way he did in "The Sandman."

"No way," I breathed, shuddering, as I closed the book and set it on my desk. "No way."

Shutting the book and turning away from it didn't rid my mind of questions, though. Talking to Brenda had cleared up a lot of things and really helped me find some comfort in knowing I wasn't alone. At the same time, she'd also raised some pretty disturbing questions about my identity and the role of free will and stuff.

IT WAS CLOSE to eight o'clock. Dinner was done, dishes cleaned up, trash taken out, homework completed. I paced around my room and then threw my window open into the night and the thin fog that now blanketed Vintage City.

I didn't fool myself into knowing for sure that Peter was going to swing by during a break from his crime-fighting. With Wade under his wing—my alliteration skills had improved, clearly—he'd likely spend time chilling out with her on some rooftop somewhere else, preferably at the opposite end of the city from where I lived. Althea hadn't contacted me in a while, too, and I knew why. It was easier to brush her off in that sense, though, seeing as how we weren't going steady. Peter, on the other hand…

I dragged my chair to the window and perched myself on it, opening Brenda's book again and mustering my focus to go back and reread "The Sandman." If Peter decided to talk to me about us, I'd be ready.

I finished the story before long, and Peter hadn't showed up. I moved on to the next story, which turned out to be a gazillion times longer and more complicated than "The Sandman." I didn't get it.

Somehow I managed to pick my way through, my brows knitting the whole time, and though I did manage to finish the story before lights out, I was still left scratching my head and wondering what these 19th century writers used to drink or smoke to come up with crazy-ass stuff like that.

In a word, I was impressed. Confused as hell, but impressed. I really should go to the public library and see if I could find more bizarre 19th century German literature. I might not understand a single damned word, but they'd make for way more fun reading compared to Hesse.

I looked back out and scanned the dark cityscape. It sucked, not seeing Peter again, not hearing from him. At the back of my mind, I'd known all along things between us would come down to that, with him drifting away because of what he was and what his role demanded of him. He'd reassured me several times before that things wouldn't change and that he loved me, yadda, yadda, yadda, despite my nagging concerns about our obvious inequality. Now with the Puppet gathering strength and Wade literally tumbling into the picture…

I carried my chair back to my desk and set the book down. It was time for bed. Before I shut the window, though, I toyed with the faintest hope that Peter might somehow be out there still. I leaned out and looked around, but no dice. Other than the usual nighttime city noise, I could hear or sense nothing, even with my enhanced hearing and vision.

"Good night, Peter," I said all the same before closing the window. When I crawled under the covers, I realized I was freezing. I guess I was too distracted by the book and by the sudden bizarre turn my life took to notice I was endangering my health.

Then again, maybe I wanted to and just didn't want to admit it. I drifted off to sleep eventually and dreamt of something I couldn't remember the following morning—but still left me feeling a touch weirded out without understanding why. I shrugged it off. At that point in time, I really should've gotten used to being unsettled and flailing in the ether.

SCREW PRIDE. I was in love with him.

After I got my stuff from my locker, I hurried over to his, pushing my way through the rest of the students to get there. I was sure Peter saw me coming. If he didn't, he sensed me at least—all those "Can we talk about this and save our relationship? I swear I'll change" vibes barreling down the corridor in his direction. Althea, who stood beside him, saw me and gave me a very uncomfortable sort of smile.

"Hi," I panted, nodding at her and grinning.

"Hey." She paused, stole a glance at Peter, who kept his back to me as he fumbled around his locker for his books, and then smiled back at me. "How's it going?"

Ugh. Small talk. I hated small talk. Especially if it was small, nervous, self-conscious talk between good friends.

"Good, good," I said. My smile was now frozen on my face, and it was beginning to hurt my muscles. I looked at Peter, who was then stuffing his backpack. "Hi, Peter."

"Hi."

Althea and I fell silent, exchanging forced grins and apologetic shrugs. I felt like an idiot.

Common sense told me to walk away before something else happened, but being the dumbass that I was, stood there, waiting for Peter to be done with his backpack despite knowing he was dragging things out on purpose so I'd grow tired or get the hint and just leave.

What the hell?

"So, uh, you guys free anytime soon, so we can hang out at the Jumping Bean or something?" I prodded. There wasn't time to think. I just blurted out what came easily.

Althea looked startled. "Oh," she said, glancing at Peter again. "I'm not sure…"

"Huh? You mean you don't know?"

"I've got homework, duh. Then there's the Puppet and all that…"

I gave her a playful punch on the shoulder. "Chrissakes, girl, how about a break from all the superhero stuff? I mean, come on! You guys deserve a breather every once in a while."

Althea punched me back. "Damn, that hurts!" she returned, but she was stifling a grin and looked more relaxed than before. "Listen, we're not done yet, Eric. We're really onto something, and we have to keep working at it. The Puppet's a hell of a lot more slippery than the Trill, you know. It's been a bitch finding leads on him. Ohmigawd, I sound so official."

"What's wrong with hanging out? It doesn't happen every day." I snorted, waving a dismissive hand, hoping I appeared totally blasé. "What's the matter? The mayor putting the hurt on you or something?"

Althea rolled her eyes. "What do you think, Sherlock? I guess you forgot about what happened downtown a few days ago."

"Screw it! How would an afternoon off from super-detective work hurt? It's been a while since we did it—like—I don't know, but it's been long enough."

Peter yanked his backpack from the floor and whirled around to face me. "Listen," he snarled, jabbing me hard on the chest with a finger. Caught off-guard, I staggered back a pace. I'd never seen him so livid: white-complexioned, his eyes flashing, his teeth clenched. His eyes were also sunken and shadowed, but I barely registered that. I was stunned speechless.

"The world doesn't revolve around *you*, Plath. The city obviously has problems on its hands, and we're the only ones who can fix things. I'm sorry we're ruining your oh-so-comfy world of coffee and stories and old books, but unlike *you*, we've got responsibilities that we never asked for. We're not thinking about ourselves when we give up all those hours that could've gone to normal shit that turns *you* on—and that we would've enjoyed. We're thinking about everyone else in the city, you know, people outside *your* snug little circle? Yeah, they actually exist, in case you haven't heard. It might be news to you, but what we do actually matters, and if we didn't do our job, you wouldn't be standing here, whining about hanging out at the Jumping Bean. You'd be in the morgue with everyone else."

"Jesus, Peter, lay off!" Althea cut in sharply, but he wasn't listening.

Peter continued to fix me with his look. I swear he could've eaten me alive on the spot. "I'm done, and I don't care who hears. I'm tired of being the one who has to be mature enough for both of us. I think it's time for us to take a break from each other, Eric. We both need space to seriously consider what we have. It's obvious we got into this too fast and without thinking. I know it's my fault for starting it, so don't bang your head against the wall over this."

Althea stared at us, shocked. I didn't know what I felt at that moment. Numbness, I guess. Horror. Humiliation. If I kept my head, I'd have said something reassuring back to keep this from moving forward, but I didn't. I just stood there, gaping at him, blushing a deep red—I was sure—and feeling sick to my stomach. Yes, like the real dumbass that I was.

It was Peter who broke the silence. "Yeah," he said, turning and heading down the hallway toward our first class. "I figured you wouldn't even have anything to say to that. Whatever. That's it."

Althea stayed behind, toeing the ground and resting her gaze on everything else but me. "Hey, I'm sorry about that," she said, her voice barely heard, after a long, awkward moment of silence. "I'm sure he didn't mean what he said."

"He's right, you know. All I've done since you guys came into your powers was to think of myself." How I managed to find my voice again, I couldn't say. "I'm really sorry, Althea."

She met my gaze, looking stricken. "For what it's worth, I miss the old times. I've got enough responsibility at home, keeping up my grades and helping out my mom. This, though, I love doing, but I hate how it's pulling me away from, like you said, normal stuff. I'd kill to have a banana split with you and Peter, you know, but I can't. At least not now. Not until we kick the Puppet's ass."

"Yeah, I know. Go on ahead," I said. I even gave her a weak pat on the shoulder. "I'll be right there. No use making you late on my account."

She didn't argue. Discomfort and mortification were written all over her face, and she turned around and walked off without another word. I watched her go and melt into the crowd of students. I wasn't aware of how long I stood there, staring at nothing while I got jostled by kids who hurried back and forth. I couldn't even remember actually walking to the classroom, but I did, even crossing the threshold just as the second bell rang. I took my seat, yeah—took out my book and my notes, yeah—but couldn't remember doing them.

I survived the day, I suppose. I found it pretty easy staying away from Peter and Althea. An illegal sandwich in the darkest corner of the library during lunch—because Ms. Mendoza had the keenest sense of smell. She could track anyone down, blind-folded, within a fifty-mile radius. I also paid a monetary bribe to switch places with Jason Sparks in our Art class. The opportun-istic jerk took the money. I didn't think he would, but I was desperate enough to sit as far away from Peter as possible, so I gambled on Jason taking pity on me when I flashed him a crumpled bill. A crummy-looking buck and a pathetic little plea; one would think he'd go, "Oh, okay, I'll switch. Keep your money." But no. Predator.

When the final bell rang, I was out of that Art Class so fast, my would-have-been-children's-had-I-been-born-heterosexual-heads spun. Good thing I'd made sure to pull out all the books I needed for homework from my locker during lunch. I didn't have to stop by there after the final bell and just fled the school grounds.

I rode my bike blindly through all kinds of side streets. I sure didn't know where I was headed, only that something bitter and nagging kept gnawing at my belly, and it was hell seeing through my tears because I finally broke down and sobbed my way through one street after another. I didn't want to go home, not yet, anyway. I guess I just wanted to ride all over the city till I collapsed from exhaustion or my bike got a flat. Besides, I was too young to get drunk—not to mention too broke and too guilt-ridden to even attempt to get my loser paws on alcohol. Of course, I could always get myself picked up by the Trill's thugs again. But no one knew where they'd gone with their boss locked away and still waiting for me to hustle my ass over there and get him out. So the thought of getting freebies in the direction of the corruption of a minor was pretty much dead in the water.

I ended up doing the next best thing: turning on the switch and playing around with my powers. Here and there, when the coast was clear, I harnessed my grief and anger and zapped un-suspecting dumpsters or mailboxes or even cars. Here and there, I cloaked—not clocked, cloaked, goddamn it!—random objects. I either partially crushed them—an exercise in subtle ninja attacks—or moved them to some bizarre location. One dumpster ended up blocking the entrance of a barber shop. One froufrou sports car got re-parked in a one-way street, facing the wrong direction with half of it on the sidewalk.

"The world can go fuck itself," I ground out, sniffling and rubbing my eyes against my damp sleeve.

Who knew how many corners I turned? I didn't even know where the hell I was, but after several minutes of random attacks, I found myself in an unfamiliar street flanked by old warehouses, some of which had been converted into hardware stores or different large retail spaces that were now abandoned.

I also found myself cycling straight into three walking mannequins: the Shadow Puppet's "men."

I'd no idea what they were doing there, but it was pretty safe to assume they were up to no good. Because, you know, supervillain toadies. They tottered, robot-like, toward me, all dressed in the usual Zoot suits, their white, blank faces all locked onto me. Even without eyes, they saw me. I felt the weight of their non-existent stares and shuddered.

I stopped and dismounted, and the red and yellow of my world intensified. The heat that had been kept to a minimum in my head grew, and it reached such a level as to make me break out in sweat, something I'd never experienced before. I knew what was coming, though, seeing as how I was the only human in the area.

Energy—hot, no longer warm—flared around me, its source pulsing in my head as I concentrated on the three mannequins. They'd stopped when I did, and with jerky but quick movements, reached inside their jacket pockets and pulled out guns.

"Bite me, jerks," I spat. "I'm just in the mood for this shit."

The first round of bullets echoed, and a hot breeze rose around me. From the cracked and grimy asphalt, it swirled upward, twisting around me in a corkscrew, carrying stray debris and dust. My hair and my clothes fluttered, and all memories of

Peter, Althea, Mom, Dad, Liz, Brenda, Mrs. Zhang—all good, loving, and familiar connections I'd clung to till then vanished.

I grinned. "Oh, it is *on*."

The swirl of hot air easily caught the bullets, and I could see those bizarre things penetrating the protective wall and stopping in mid-flight, only to be swept up, harmless, and thrown off to the side. The mannequins kept shooting at me, and I let them exhaust their weapons. Idiots. Then again mannequins didn't have brains, so yay, me.

"Walking dolls are stupid." I laughed. "Why would anyone want these losers to do all the dirty work for them?" They'd run out of ammo, and all I could hear were useless clicks as they kept pulling the triggers.

Undaunted, they threw their guns away and marched toward me. Sure, whatever. Still laughing, I stopped the swirling air and let loose a blast of energy that shot them all down, tearing their Italian suits, leaving burn marks on their faces. They crumpled to the ground and lay quivering for a few seconds before struggling back up. It was just like the downtown attacks, with the mannequins coming back again and again till they were literally torn apart or incinerated.

I suppose on one level they were an inspiration to anyone who'd give up so quickly. On the other, I still thought they were just dumb machines.

I needed the practice, anyway. Battered but still whole, the trio got to their wooden feet and continued to march toward me. I leaped out of their way, flying toward a stack of wooden crates nearby and leaving a visible energy wave in my wake as I landed on—or, rather, floated above—the topmost crate. They turned to follow me, and that was when I realized a few more walking mannequins were emerging from the shadows, from behind rotting boxes, dumpsters, and out of a narrow door that led to a dilapidated warehouse, which was more of a rotting, half-burned shell. Each had a tommy gun, ready and aimed.

Human Swiss cheese, anyone? Yeah, fun times.

CHAPTER 19

I ROLLED MY eyes. The energy cloud that cloaked me flickered and pulsed, shooting up like a candle's flame. I felt the surge of power that came with that, and I didn't even have to think about it. I seemed to have reached a point where my powers just plain reacted to my body's responses to the situation I was in. My powers and I were finally in sync.

I watched the first three mannequins stagger closer, while the new arrivals marched in my direction, aiming their weapons. For a moment, I wondered why they were there, lying as though in ambush, unless…

More energy pulsed around me just as the new arrivals started shooting.

…unless they were expecting someone else. Magnifiman, maybe? Calais? Miss Pyro? Any of the superheroes or maybe all of them?

Bullets flew all over the place, hitting boxes, brick walls, pavement, but none got me. My energy cloak ate them all this time, holding them suspended in its thick heat for a second before melting them till nothing was left, and new bullets took their place.

I moved my arms away from my body, my palms facing outward. No, I didn't even have to think about this one, either. Suddenly my hands vanished in a pulsing cloud of yellow and red. I narrowed my eyes as heat intensified in my head. I let loose a fierce wave of hot energy from my forehead and both my hands. I cried out—a war cry, almost—every ounce of anger, bitterness, resentment, and defiance pouring out of my system in that one shrill scream.

My hair and my clothes fluttered wildly. I watched three rolling, unstoppable waves flow out in a rapid and widening fan, overlapping at a certain point and literally mowing down every single mannequin they swept over. Noise filled my ears, a low rumbling like an earthquake, the sounds of wood and plastic cracking, of fabric being torn to ribbons.

I stopped my attack when I couldn't hear bullets being fired.

The waves faded, and the scene cleared. I stared, totally amazed, at the carnage before me. Mannequins lay all over the grimy asphalt, some completely destroyed, most still functioning but damaged. Like the first three that had attacked me, they were partly burned, their costumes tattered or missing parts, their movements jerky but determined as they struggled to raise themselves up from where they lay. Their weapons were strewn around them, mostly mangled, with faint black smoke rising from broken parts and not just the barrels.

"Want more, huh?"

My hands flared up again, and this time I leaped off the crates and flew above them, turning myself around like a cat in mid-air and blasting them with more energy waves before all of them were on their feet.

"Eat that!"

Had I been a helpless bystander, I probably would've freaked out over the rumbling noise alone, but it was music to me. My breath caught, my skin prickled, and the feeling of listening to my favorite song swept over me—an amazing sensation that was edged with a strong shade of destruction. The blending of opposites was just beautiful.

Below me, the scene was once again blanketed with waves that distorted physical surfaces the way heat waves did. In the midst of all this, I could see outlines of mannequins writhing and falling over in the blast.

I landed several feet away, this time keeping my feet firmly planted on the ground while I surveyed the damage. Most of the mannequins were destroyed. There were still about four that were barely hanging on. Like the brainless machines that they were, they tried to get back on their feet, failing and toppling back down because they were either missing body parts or their limbs were crooked or non-functioning. They were pretty determined, though. I had to give them that.

But I got them, and I got them good. Of course, I was also slowly growing aware of fatigue. My powers had limits or something? I didn't know that, and I sure as hell hoped not! I whirled around at the sound of furtive scuttling behind me, my powers pulsing back to life, and I was once again cocooned in hazy warmth.

"What the hell?" a voice bleated. "I thought you were on our side!"

From another stack of rotting crates, a figure emerged—peeked out for a moment, that is, and then crept out. As it walked toward me, two more figures appeared. They were tiny ones, this time, like shrunken people. But their appearance left no doubt in my mind they were marionettes that moved on their own. I'd seen marionettes on TV before. Trust me, these were marionettes. Only independently moving in that seriously mental way.

I pursed my lips and racked my brain. How did supervillains greet each other when meeting for the first time? Greetings and salutations? Well met, stranger? Hey, dude? Ah, it's finally come to this? It's an honor, sir?

The trio stopped, and I sighed, shrugging.

"Yo," I said. "What's up?"

The Puppet looked me over—I think. It was hard to say exactly where his eyes were going, seeing as how the face I was looking at wasn't a real face, but a white image of one projected against a black screen. All right, let me back track here.

The puppet was a pretty short guy. Doll-like? No, screw the pun. He was short and skinny, and he wore a black bodysuit that covered everything, and I mean everything. Head, face, torso, arms, hands, legs, and feet. Everything was encased in black spandex that shimmered slightly in the sunlight. The fabric was obviously not thick enough to keep him from seeing me, hearing me, or even breathing and talking. What weirded me out was the face projected on the black blankness of his spandex-covered head. It was white, with the features in hazy black. The face itself was a little larger than what the Puppet's real face must be. The projected image filled the entire front of the Puppet's covered face, so there was an obvious disproportion from the viewer's perspective. It was almost like the Puppet was all face and very little body. The face also flickered or lost focus every so often, just like the way those old projectors in movie houses used to flicker and show dirt and scratches on the images against the screen.

"Hey, what's wrong with your face? I mean—how'd you do that?" I blurted out, sincerely puzzled. I resisted looking over my shoulder and checking to see where the projector might be hidden because I didn't want to open myself up to possible attacks from the Puppet's demon marionettes.

Speaking of marionettes, did I mention those things looked like the ones used in that old, cheesy, 60s puppet sci-fi series, *Thunderbirds*? Dad had taped a few episodes some time ago. He'd held onto those VHS recordings for dear life till the tape jammed the old VCR with yards of tangled ribbon. The marionettes were sort of like Mini-Me, but wooden. With Ken Doll hairdos. And elaborate silk and lace costumes that reminded me of masquerades. What a bizarre trio they made—but I must admit I couldn't help but admire the costumes; whoever worked on those dolls' togs was a master craftsman. The Puppet noticed my interest.

"Today's Casanova Day," he said, nodding at his assistants. He sounded pretty young. In fact, I wouldn't be surprised if he turned out to be my age, if not a year or two older.

"Tomorrow, it's Joan of Arc Day, and they'll be in armor. The day after that, it's Madonna."

"No shit." I was doubly impressed. How loaded was this guy? "Are you—"

"I'm not gay. God, talk about stereotyping."

"I was going to ask about the costumes and whether or not you're a tailor or something. Jeez, talk about defensive! Oh, and before you hit me with anything homophobic, I'm gay—100% prime, government disapproved. And I can kick your puny ass if you say the f-word." My energy cloak pulsed in emphasis.

"So what's this? Internalized homophobia?" he snorted. "Are you projecting on to me?"

I rolled my eyes. Somehow I felt I'd be better off holding a conversation with my toenail clippings. "I'm sorry I brought anything up. Anyway, you haven't answered my question about your face."

"Yeah, well that was pretty rude. I'd kick your ass right now if my mannequins weren't blown up. And, no, I'm not going to tell you my secrets. Get your own special effects."

I rubbed the back of my neck. "Why can't you fight? That's pretty lame, depending on your dolls to destroy things. And, yeah, I'm on your side, but what did you expect me to do when your stupid mannequins started shooting at me? Stand there, flash them, and hope my dick would calm them down?"

"Hey, listen. My powers are in here," he retorted, poking a spandex-covered finger against his head. "I'm a freakin' genius, and I made these mannequins from scratch, and not even Magnifiman and his wimpy gang can figure me out! You've seen the way my dolls fight. They're practically indestructible!"

"Uh, 'practically' isn't exactly very reassuring." I jerked my head in the direction of the steaming piles of quivering wood and plastic, some of which were still trying to stand up but could only go as far as jerk, writhe, and spasm on the ground.

The two marionettes shifted on their froufrou feet, exchanging wooden glances before gazing back up at me. If they'd had voices, I was sure they'd be muttering all kinds of threats.

The Puppet snorted, resting his hands on his hips. "Hello? It didn't take me long to reach this stage of my development. Can't say that about the Trill, can we? Experiments here and there, hoodlums who could barely make it from Point A to Point B—made of fail, dude. Then again, that's what you get for hiring human thugs for your cabal."

I smirked. I couldn't help it. "You're pretty cool. I like you. If I weren't tied to the Trill, I'd actually work with you as your partner or something. Like that Riker guy on Star Trek."

The two marionettes took a few steps closer, raising their gloved fists in the air—like threatening gestures, I thought. Did they seriously think they could take me on? I'd squash them both into instant woodchips before they'd take another step forward.

"Too bad. The sidekick position's already filled twice over, and my kids don't really care to be replaced. Oi! Back!"

The two mini-thugs backed away and took their places again, but I sensed an undercurrent of anger from them. Talk about bizarre all the way. They actually felt something, and they were sending out those vibes to me. Oooohh, gee, how scary. I was *so* shaking in my sneakers.

"So what were those mannequins doing, hiding behind boxes and stuff and then jumping me without any reason?"

"They were waiting for someone else, but you shot everything to hell. Thanks a lot, jerk."

"An ambush then! I knew it! Who were they waiting for? Magnifiman?"

"Duh?"

I looked around me, slightly intensifying my energy cloak.

"The tables can be turned in their favor if we stand here long enough, yammering away."

The white face contorted into shock before fixing an expression of angry caution on its flickering features. "Crap. I gotta go." He turned and pointed a threatening finger at me, his overlarge face showing irritation. "Now I have to go back and assemble a new host of killing dolls—again, no thanks to you! I had my plan all laid out perfectly, too, but you had to show up and screw things up. I have to start over and waste time!"

I shrugged. "Hey, look, it was bad timing all around. I sure as hell wasn't planning on coming here, and I didn't expect your killing dolls to be lurking around dumpsters."

"Yeah, well, you came too early. I just sent Magnifiman some coded warnings, and he was supposed to show up here, uh, once he figured things out. Screw it. I'm not wasting more time talking to you. I'm going."

"Like your dumb dolls would've mattered, considering who they're up against." So much for being a "freakin' genius".

He gave me the middle finger and then a low whistle. The marionettes turned on their heels and ran off, diving behind the same pile of crates where they'd hidden themselves at first. What the hell were they doing?

Ensuring foolproof protection from the superheroes when they showed up? I shook my head. Stupid dolls.

"Hey, want to touch base again sometime?" I asked, taking a couple of cautious looks around to make sure we were still alone. "Maybe we can come up with a really good World Domination scheme. I can contribute something. I've played Risk with my sister before, and I know how to be a good strategist. I've beaten her, seven out of ten. Wanna do it?"

The Puppet laughed and waved me off. "I work alone," he said. "Nice try, loser."

"Liar. You've got a harem of killing dolls. I don't call that alone."

"Yeah, well, I don't need your help. If you're aligned with

the Trill, you'd better not screw around with your loyalties. That's one of the first things you need to know. The Supervillain Handbook says so."

He turned around and hurried back to the same spot where his assistants hid themselves.

"I don't think it's a good idea hiding from Magnifiman that way!" I called out.

"What way?" he called back without a glance back at me or a slowing down of his pace.

Just before I could say another word, the sudden explosive sputtering of an engine broke the silence. The Puppet leaped up—he could do flying leaps like me and all the other heroes and villains; that was the only thing that we all had in common, I guess—landing on the ground and springing up a couple of times before sailing over the pile of crates and vanishing behind them.

Within seconds, the engine sound swelled with several deafening pops as someone revved it. A black, shiny, uber-tricked out motorcycle sped out from behind the crates.

Or so I hoped.

Actually, it was a moped. No, wait. It was a Vespa. The leather saddle made me think it was a vintage design, if not an actual scooter from the 60s. The Puppet was on it, his identity protected by a helmet, and he drove off pretty quickly. His "kids" sat on the seat behind him—yes, happily protected from the hazards of the road with their own teeny, custom-made bike helmets.

"I wonder if they have helmets for every day of the week?" I mused, scratching my head.

I stopped and held my breath. My über acute hearing caught the distant sounds of abnormal air disturbances, which could only mean one thing. Magnifiman and the gang were flying toward the warehouses, just as the Puppet had planned.

The good side to having über acute hearing was that I was easily warned. The bad side was that there was no way for me to know exactly how close they were. All the same, I sure as hell wasn't going to stay around to know how good my sensing was.

I rose and flew into one of the open warehouse doors, trusting to my cloaking powers' ability to—ayup, cloak me—from the others' sensory powers temporarily, at least.

The warehouse was a mess of abandoned crap. There was no light, either, and I didn't have the advantage of acute night vision.

"Damn it," I hissed, looking around me.

Faint voices could be heard from outside somewhere, two male and one female. The superheroes were there. I needed to get out or face them all, one against three. Althea must be at home or at the Barlows' or maybe even the police station, already hooked up to the computer.

They gradually grew louder, and I could make out bits of the conversation.

"Holy shit!" a young male voice—Peter's, I recognized—exclaimed. "What the hell happened here?"

Another male voice, Trent's, obviously, said something I couldn't hear clearly. A female voice joined in, sounding excited. I caught "a trap" and "an ambush" from her. There was a brief pause before I heard another exclamation from Peter. Wade spoke, and I heard her mention something about a "bicycle." A hurried conversation followed, and I turned my attention away.

Peter had seen my bike lying on the ground, just a few feet from the pile of mangled mannequins. I kept myself from bitterly laughing out loud. I quietly flew around the warehouse, taking care to avoid bumping against things. The voices continued behind me. Judging from their consistently low volume, I guessed they weren't moving toward the warehouse. All the same, I didn't want to take a chance.

I spotted a window that was completely devoid of glass. Around it the other windows were either whole and caked with filth or broken in places, the openings not large enough for me to squeeze through. I immediately flew to the open one, relieved at the silence my powers gave my movements. Aiming well, I shot through the hole…

…and immediately thumped hard against a wall of solid

muscle, a breathless "Oof!" puffing out of me.

Hands, large, strong, and very familiar, grabbed my jacket and yanked me up till I half-hung, half-floated outside the warehouse, staring right into Magnifiman's narrowed eyes.

"I've got you now, you little pipsqueak," he snarled. "It's curtains for you and your devious—"

He stopped, confusion momentarily shadowing his perfect, chiseled features.

There was no turning back now. Whatever Brenda had said about choices and free will being a part of my experiences as an "Olympia," sure didn't apply to me. I was manipulated into becoming something, and what I did when my powers were on felt like it had nothing to do with free will. Action-reaction. Anger—there was so much of it boiling in me, feeding my powers.

I went for broke.

"What's up?" I said, smirking at the shock that now registered on Magnifiman's face.

"You!" he cried.

"Surprise!"

We were all newbies at this, I suppose. Magnifiman let his guard down for a few seconds—not very smart—and I took advantage of it. I focused—concentrated—used up as much reserve as I could. The red and yellow of my world brightened, brightened, brightened, till I was sure I was going to be blinded. Heat from the deepest pit in my belly flared and coursed out.

There was a flash—a massive, painful explosion of energy—and I was torn from Magnifiman's grip, tumbling in space backward, while he was thrown in the opposite direction.

CHAPTER 20

THAT SURE WASN'T a good way to treat one's kinda-sorta-brother-in-law, but then again, there was no hard and fast rules involving one's kinda-sorta-ex-brother-in-law. The energy blast knocked me well out of Magnifiman's reach, and though I was dizzy from all the tumbling, something in me held fast, kept me from losing all my focus despite my crazy situation.

Somehow, while rolling in space, I managed to take advantage of the momentum caused by my energy wave and used it to catapult myself farther away from the warehouse.

I really didn't know where I was going. I was only aware of losing all sense of direction, completely unclear as to whether or not I was upright or not, and whether or not I was flying up or falling down. I just felt this frightening and uncontrollable forward push, with my body instinctively positioning itself as I rode the last wave of energy that was taking me away from Magnifiman. I guess it was like body surfing in warm, rolling air. Maybe it was all instinct and self-preservation completely taking over.

"There!" someone shouted somewhere.

I forced my eyes open and found myself sailing clear above

another warehouse. I was flying for real. I glanced over my shoulder and caught sight of a fiery streak following me.

"Great," I hissed. "Wade."

I made a sharp turn when the sound of Wade's flight grew more distinct: the whoosh of air around her, the crackling of fire as she channeled her powers. Bearing left, I made for a giant billboard that was perched atop one dilapidated building. The billboard was really nothing more than a rusty rectangular steel frame with a discolored and tattered vinyl sheet flapping weakly in the breeze. I took my place on it, turning around to face my approaching enemy. Balancing on that steel frame as it groaned and moved under my weight was a cakewalk. My powers and my quick mastery of them continued to amaze me.

"Go on!" I called out, raising my arms from my sides like before as the energy surged from the pit of my stomach through every inch of my body till I felt like a dam that had just been riddled with holes. "Let's see what you got!"

Wade stopped and hovered in space, the fire that initially covered her vanishing. She faced me with a look of intense concentration mixed with anger. Without taking her eyes off me, she raised one arm and extended it, her fire whip bursting out of her palm and shooting out like a fiery tentacle. Within seconds, she'd closed her fingers around its handle. It hung in space, waiting to be used. Fire ran along the length of the weapon.

For a moment, we challenged each other in a battle of wills of kinds. Like a staring contest, waiting for the first one to blink.

"You're not getting away this time," she called out, finally. Her voice was light and very girly, the kind of voice that one might expect to hear from a young, shy bookworm type. It was a voice that didn't evoke a lot of strength, but I knew better than to underestimate her, given who'd mentored her, and continued to mentor her, for that matter.

"So where's your boyfriend?" I asked, my heart racing, the bile in my stomach surging at every word. "Abandoned you, did he?"

She grinned, not once contradicting me. Wade had definitely

improved by way of confidence since I last saw her. I could sense a kind of hunger there, an eagerness to break me where I stood.

In fact, I even caught sight of her fingers working on the handle of her fire whip, loosening and tightening around it as if she were kneading, but it definitely spoke volumes of her holding herself in check for the moment. It was like watching a spring compacting itself in a tight coil, ready for a sudden, violent release.

I braced myself, matching her will for will. My heart continued to thunder against my ribs.

"Calais has better things to do than stay around for you."

"So he left you to deal with garbage, eh? Not exactly a very equal relationship."

Wade swung her arm, snapping her fire whip with a loud cry. I instinctively raised an arm to ward off the blow, and my energy cloak softened it—slowed it down. The whip's end cut into the thick warmth and coiled around my arm. Its momentum and impact reduced, it uncoiled in a second and slipped off just as Wade yanked it back.

The fire whip flew out, trailing fire in the air as it snapped back without me attached to it.

Wade let out a gasp of anger. With her free hand, she aimed and shot me a series of fireballs—about a dozen at least in rapid succession. I could hear the rhythmic Choom! Choom! that followed them. I countered her attack with an energy blast. It tore through the air in a high speed beam, colliding with Wade's fireballs midway and setting off brilliant explosions of energy and flames between us.

I followed that with another blast, taking advantage of the momentary confusion caused by the explosions. Wade managed to leap out of the way, though, and my energy blast tore into a pile of old crates on the warehouse's roof that was behind her.

"Not bad for garbage!" she cried, snapping her whip as she flew up, this time aiming for my feet. She missed them, but her whip coiled around the steel frame I stood on, heating it within seconds. The rusty frame turned red and began to smoke. I flew up before I got roasted, refocusing my powers, feeding off my resentment toward Wade. Before she could snap her whip back, I let loose one more energy wave. It shot through the air in a violent rippling current. She saw it, tried to leap out of the way, but was caught in its flow and carried off. I watched it throw her against a collection of old steel drums that sat rotting on another warehouse's roof. She crashed against them with a shout as drums flew all over.

"Yeah, not bad for garbage, huh?" I sneered.

"You there!"

I turned and saw Magnifiman hovering just to my right. He raised both hands out to me. Heat in my belly churned again, pulsing and growing, readying itself for the next volley.

"You don't have to do this!" he cried. "Listen to me— you're not one of us!"

"No, I never was. I never will be," I snarled.

"No one wants to hurt you."

"Seriously? Gee, how ironic," I spat. Hurt me? He'd no idea. Seriously absolutely *no* idea. "Spare me any speeches about justice and peace and equality and all that junk, either. Whatever you tell me has been programmed into you. You're hardwired into talking like a comic book character, and I'll bet you don't mean a word you say."

He ignored me, and I could see his body tensing up, readying itself, even though his voice stayed calm and steady. "Listen. You're a good kid. I know you are. Let me help you. Let us help you and bring whoever did this to you to justice."

I sprang back, leaping across the way and onto the next rooftop when Magnifiman suddenly flew at me. His arms embraced air as he sailed over where I'd stood a second earlier. Close behind him flew Wade, her fire whip gone, but she'd flared up again, her body outlined by fire. She took her place beside Magnifiman and faced me, this time poised for action with her fists raised at her sides. I don't want to admit this, but she looked absolutely breathtaking like that, and I hated her even more for it. A strong girl. A very smart one, according to Peter, nice and sweet behind all that power. She was also straighter than a straight line. I couldn't even begin to imagine all the things she could offer to any family who'd take her into the fold. Together, they might work their influence on Peter and coax him into a closeted future that was completely free of me and all the economic, intellectual, and identity baggage that came with my miserable four-eyed self. All those reassurances Peter kept feeding me—"Don't worry this, don't worry that, blah, blah, blah"—who the hell was he trying to bullshit?

"Too late for that," I yelled. It was all too much for me to deal with. I was close to breaking down again. "Too late for anything! I warned you all before. No one listened. Hell, no one believed me! Chalk my nightmares up to post-traumatic stress, right? My head wasn't raped, right? The only thing the Trill did was to screw around with me and make me believe I was programmed to follow instructions. Pretty easy explanation, wasn't it?"

Where the hell was Peter? He should be there, watching me, seeing his own handiwork. Yeah, I blamed him. He was the one who fed me all the crap about trauma and the Trill being no better than they were, being a bumbling newbie like everyone else. What bull it turned out to be. This was Peter's fault. All his fault. It could've been stopped a long time ago, with proper help, considering the technology the superheroes had access to.

But no. The Devil's Trill was a newbie, he said. The Devil's Trill couldn't possibly reach inside my head and plant himself there, he said. No way, he said. No way.

"So what do you want?" Wade called out. "You want to be hurt? Is that it?"

"Hurt? Hurt?" I laughed. "What the hell do you know about me, anyway?"

"More than you know," she returned.

"Yeah, I'll fucking bet you do."

"Enough of this," Magnifiman cut in. He launched himself at me.

Heat and thick, asphyxiating air flared up around me. "Yeah, enough of this," I ground out. Red and yellow intensified, brightened. All I could make out were vague silhouettes of Magnifiman flying toward me, with Wade at his side. The silhouettes melted in the spiraling whiteness that suddenly blinded me, and I shouted as hot energy exploded from my body—a cloud of distortion and swirling colors and pent-up rage.

I couldn't see Magnifiman and Wade as they flew right into the massive cloud. I didn't think they'd be completely damaged by it, but I knew I'd just bought myself enough time to escape.

I turned and flew off the roof, spent and in pain from the violence of my efforts. I took the direction of the asylum, the fury that had just found release still eating away at me as I landed on one rooftop after another. I glowed as I went. A glance or two at my limbs and my clothes showed that I was physically pulsing with energy from deep within. I must look like a white ball that bounced off the tops of buildings. In the process of escape, I sent volley after volley of waves, all randomly directed. Windows blew in, bricks exploded from the walls of tenements, grimy light bulbs on billboards or street lamps burst in a shower of broken glass. Junk collected on abandoned rooftops flew out and disappeared into the streets. Here and there I could hear people shouting as debris rained on them below.

I expected to be caught by Magnifiman at any time, but I didn't hear anyone pursuing me. All right, then, was I being saved for someone else?

I paused at one point, catching my breath as I crouched on the roof of a terraced house in a familiar street. I shook like crazy under the strain of seriously jacked up emotions and powers, panting as I watched an old house across the street from where I'd perched myself.

My bedroom window was thrown open. The light was on, and I could see a part of my bed. Farther down, the light was also turned on in my parents' bedroom. They were all home now, and I imagined how they were going about their business behind those weathered brick walls—what they talked about, where they gathered, the tone of their voices as they wondered about me. I should've been home a long time ago.

"I'm here, Mom, Dad. Across the street. Just look out the window, and you'll see me."

A silhouette moved past the window on the bottom floor, next to the front door. Someone was in the living room, probably watching the news. Probably using the phone. I forced myself to look away, a small sound escaping my tight throat, and I reminded myself of what I needed to do.

The asylum was at the other end of the city, I told myself. There was no time for anything else. I flew off, managing to clear three more rooftops.

Then I hit something, or something hit me. The world spun, melted in a streak of confused colors and shapes. My stomach lurched as the city sped past me, and I clung to the arms that held me tight.

I fought and clawed my way back to some semblance of control and mustered as much energy as I could despite my weakening hold. I pinched my eyes shut, bent all thought on the swirling heat that continued to radiate from my belly.

"Get the hell off me!" I shrieked as I let loose a torrent of energy. I felt the arms around me slacken their hold, but they didn't let me go. The speed of our flight weakened, though, and the dizziness and nausea vanished. I took a moment to gather myself before struggling furiously.

I felt us descend and then crash against something wooden. Stars exploded before my eyes, and I felt jolts of pain up and down my body. My energy cloak failed to cushion our fall adequately, and I cursed myself for letting out such a weak surge. We rolled among piles of junk and came to a stop amid battered crates and boxes.

I lay on my back, panting. I opened my eyes and met Peter's gaze as he held me down with his weight.

"Eric," he breathed. I could barely hear him. "My God,

what happened to you?"

"A lot of things," I whispered back. "Good thing you broke up with me, huh?"

Peter visibly winced. "I want to help you. Trust me…"

"Again?" I snapped. The heat in me rose. "The way I trusted you when you said nothing was wrong with my head after the Trill got me?"

"Listen, Eric, please. You're not hardwired like me. What you have can be reversed."

"Oh, you mean you've figured everything out already? Just like that? Boy, I'm impressed. You did better with me than with the Puppet."

Somehow I'd managed to yank one of my arms free of his hold. Then I hauled and punched him hard on the jaw, sending him toppling off me. I stumbled to my feet despite the soreness all over my body and the exhaustion that was steadily growing. The good thing about fighting someone one used to be romantically involved with was that one could take advantage of any soft spots his ex-turned-enemy might still harbor for him.

I stood several feet away and re-energized while Peter stumbled to his feet. He turned to me, and I saw a reddish mark forming on his jaw. I thought he wouldn't be susceptible to physical bruising given his powers, but apparently I was wrong. Then again, maybe it was a sign we were evenly matched, and that gave me hope.

"What the hell do you care, anyway?" I demanded.

"Why do I need to justify myself to you?"

I laughed. "Oh, that's precious. After what you said to me this morning? Yeah—real precious."

"Eric—Eric, I'm sorry. I wasn't—"

"Fuck you, Peter."

Peter launched himself at me with a cry, swinging his arm and hitting me on the jaw. Tit for tat. I fell back and slid across the roof, my back scraping against the rough surface and the smaller debris that littered it.

"Don't make me fight you," he panted as I struggled to get up.

I rubbed the back of my hand against my lower lip and saw blood smeared across my glowing knuckles. I looked at him, my eyes narrowed, my body heaving from our exertions. Around me heat thickened.

"This is all your fault," I said. I couldn't control the violent shaking in my voice. "It's all your fault. I hope you can live with this, Barlow. Because I sure as hell won't make you forget."

Peter actually looked helpless against my insane levels of rage. It was like every word I said hit a bull's eye, and I was glad yet totally devastated.

"Your powers—they're not permanent. They can be reversed. Eric, please listen to me."

I shook my head. "I'm listening to a broken record," I hissed, and in another flash, Peter and I were rolling around in a tangle of limbs. We grappled, throwing punches, or at least I did, mostly.

He held back, dodging my fist or deflecting my hits with his arms. He punched me back a few times, which made me snap. He tried several times to pin my wrists down, but I fought like a madman. I think I *was* crazy at that moment. I managed to throw one final punch, and he was forced to tear himself away, landing a safe distance from me while I scrambled to my feet again.

We were both bruised and bleeding, our breathing ragged and loud as we continued to face off.

"Damn it, Eric, listen to me!" he cried. "I don't want to fight you!"

Thank God for giving me that advantage. I let loose a wave that swept him up before he could dodge it. "You lied to me before, Peter! What makes you think I'll believe you now?" I cried as I shot another wave after him, doubling the force of the first and pushing him off the edge of the roof.

Peter struggled against the rippling currents that held him fast. He gritted his teeth and fought as he sailed to the edge and then past it till he hovered several stories above the street. With a hoarse cry, I shot him another cloaking ball of energy—a massive one. It rolled across in a speed that surprised even me, catching Peter in its bubble before moving onward, in the direction of God knew where. I let loose another energy wave that followed the bubble, pushing it with greater speed away from me. I could barely see Peter's silhouette inside, struggling and flailing in the thick, airless warmth that surrounded him as the bubble sailed away. I sank to my hands and knees, drained, sick, and wishing I could just lie down and die right there.

From some indeterminate location, I heard the familiar sound of gunfire—endless rounds from tommy guns. The Puppet had re-emerged, I guess, with another army of killer mannequins. They must have just come face-to-face with Magnifiman and Wade back there. I silently thanked the Puppet for the diversion.

The asylum. I forced myself to get back on my feet. I flew, bending all my will and using every last ounce of my energy in the direction of the asylum, where the Trill waited for me. I felt like a battered old toy—weak, tired, bleeding, maybe broken in some places. I knew I'd screwed around long enough and that I couldn't move forward without proper guidance and help.

Time was a blur of a nanosecond. One minute, I was watching Peter—the quiet, overachieving, artistic boy I still loved—being thrown away in a suffocating energy bubble of my making. The next, I was soaking the iron bars of the Trill's windows with my energy waves, softening them, and tearing them off with my bruised and aching hands. Within seconds I was face-to-face with the Trill. A white, gaunt face stripped of its mask grinned its pride as it watched me shred the skin of my hands while I ripped the bars off.

"Listen," I began, forcing him to pause in the middle of climbing over the window ledge. "I'm coming with you, and I'll do what you want me to do as long as you stay away from my family. You got that?"

"Are you bargaining with me, young man?"

"Shut up. Either you stay away from my family, or I'll kill

you right now."

He watched me in silence. Then he grinned and laughed—long and hard, a maniacal shriek—the same kind of laughter I'd heard when he'd blown up the aerial tracks several weeks earlier.

"You've absolutely no leverage to use against me, Mr. Plath. None. Your powers are new, and you haven't even mastered them yet. If anyone does the crushing around here, that would be me. Do you understand that? But I'm tickled by your spunk, and I'll accept your terms. Your family's safe while you stay with me. Not that it would've mattered, you know. My fight's with much bigger fish than a piddling group of no-name, mediocre folks living in a sad section of the city." He took a deep breath and then sighed happily. "Unless you have other petulant demands to make, it's time you honor your end of the bargain."

I helped him out of the window, and he paused as he held on to me. His eyes narrowed as they swept over my face. He shook his head and clucked his tongue. Then he raised a hand and lightly touched my cheek with cold, white fingers.

"It seems that I failed to disconnect feeling." He sighed. "The Noxious Nocturne could only fix so many things, alas. I suppose I ought to make a few more adjustments to the program." Then he let go and flew off, still in his asylum clothes. "Let's go home, my dear boy," he called out.

I flew after him, puzzled by what he'd just said. The rush of wind around us felt icy against my face, and I touched my cheek the way the Trill had. I drew my hand back and saw it was wet with tears.

ABOUT THE AUTHOR

I'VE LIVED MOST of my life in the San Francisco Bay Area though I wasn't born there (or, indeed, the USA). I'm married with no kids and three cats, am a cycling nut, and my day job involves artwork, crazy coworkers who specialize in all kinds of media, and the occasional strange customer requests involving papier mache fish with sparkly scales.

I'm a writer of young adult fiction, specializing in contemporary fantasy, historical fantasy, and historical fiction genres. My books range from a superhero fantasy series to reworked folktales to Victorian ghost fiction.

My themes are coming-of-age, with very little focus on romance (most of the time) and more on individual growth and some adventure thrown in. More information can be found online at haydenthorne.com.

CPSIA information can be obtained at www.ICGtesting.com
Printed in the USA
LVOW05s1351141014

408702LV00001B/137/P